PREDATOR & PREY: WEREWOLF

BOOK THREE OF SIX

I0630855

Based on
WEREWOLF: THE APOCALYPSE

By Gherbod Fleming

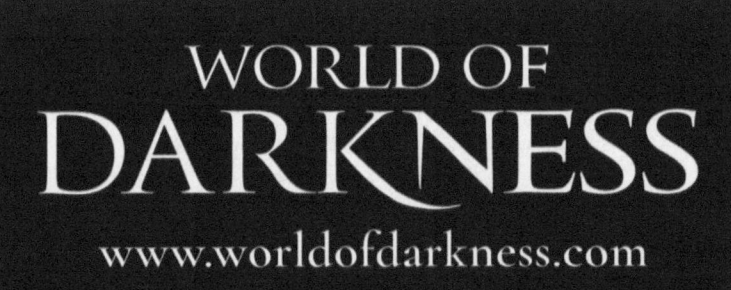

PART ONE

Chapter 1

The shot glass slid along the highly polished pine toward the customer at the end of the bar. He watched the glass's approach with unconcealed trepidation. When it came within six inches of the edge of the bar without having slowed noticeably, he fumbled for it with his thick-fingered, grimy hand, stopping the glass and spilling but a single drop of the golden-brown whiskey.

"Losin' your touch," he grumbled. *Touch* was a tricky word after so many drinks: The hard *t* sent droplets of spittle onto the spotless bar, and the *ch* was too soft, more a *sh*.

"Losing my tush?" the bartender said. "Hell with you. Wouldn't have spilled a drop if you hadn't got in the way."

"Woulda gone in the floor."

"Hell with you." The bartender with his dark hair and beard trimmed short and neat was as fastidious as his lone customer was slovenly and drunk. The reek of the unwashed man filled the tiny establishment. The bartender would have cared more if there were other patrons, or if there were likely to be. But not this late, not this far out on the edge of town. "Wouldn't have spilled a drop."

"In the floor."

"Hell with you, Hunch."

The drunk turned up his glass. The motion briefly accentuated the unsightly curvature of his spine that forced his right shoulder blade up and out, resembling a hump, though in truth the protrusion was almost as much a matter of posture and skeletal alignment as extraneous flesh. Still, to the casual observer, the drunk could be—and often was—quite reasonably labeled a hunchback.

"Hell with *you*," Hunch spat.

Their discourse was interrupted by approaching headlights shining through the front window that sported the blinking beer sign. The bartender squinted. Hunch stared into the bottom of his empty glass. Passersby were unusual enough, but what was more unusual was that this vehicle did not pass by; it slowed and turned left onto the gravel parking lot. The headlights were set high, a pickup. The bartender went back to scooping ice from the ice bin into the sink, the task that had occupied him before Hunch demanded another drink.

Truck doors slamming. Gravel-crunching footsteps. The front door opened with a blast of north-central Michigan January.

"Evening," the bartender said to the two new arrivals.

The first was a scrawny, bug-eyed excuse for a man; the second nearly had to duck to get through the door. "Evening yourself," said the scrawny one with a sneer. "You still open?"

"Open I am," the bartender said. "And with a thriving, vivacious, intellectually demanding clientele. I must have gone to church last Sunday."

"Yeah, whatever," the scrawny man said. "Two beers. What have you got on tap?"

"Not a damn thing. Tap's busted."

The scrawny man frowned; his face screwed up like a rotting pumpkin. "Sign says this is a Tap House."

"Say anything about the tap working?"

"Jeez."

"I've got bottled beer, and I got whiskey."

The big man plopped down on a barstool and wrinkled his nose. "Something die in here?"

The scrawny fellow, still standing, slapped his friend on the shoulder and pointed a thumb toward Hunch. The bar seemed cramped suddenly, crowded as it was with three customers at once, and one of them evidently not having bathed in weeks. "Hey, you," the scrawny man said to the unresponsive Hunch, "why don't you go outside and roll in something? You'll smell better."

The bartender leaned forward over the bar. "Now don't you go bothering my—"

"Yeah, yeah, whatever. Two *bottled* beers. Best of whatever you got. You got imports?"

The bartender took a deep breath. He bent down to the icebox. "Yep. Imported all the way from St. Louis."

"Jeez, what a gyp."

"Hey, you," the big guy said, calling down to Hunch, "you stink. You know that? You stink. Bad."

"You Murphy?" the scrawny one asked the bartender. "Of Murphy's Tap House? Or is the sign wrong about that too?"

"Ryan Murphy I am."

"That Irish?"

"That would seem to explain the shamrock on the sign."

"You don't sound Irish."

"A few generations among the barbarians will do that," Murphy said. "Probably several generations back *you* had an ancestor who wasn't a raving prick, but I'd never have guessed." Murphy set two bottles of beer firmly on the bar. He opened them. "Now, I suggest, gentlemen, that you drink your beer, leave me six bucks, don't bother with the tip—somehow you don't seem like the tipping sort—and then get the hell out of my bar."

The big man chuckled. "He called you a prick."

The scrawny fellow snatched the beer from the bar. He looked as if he might have chewed the cap off the bottle if Murphy hadn't already opened it.

"Hey, stinkman," the big guy said, "why don't you take a bath?"

Hunch stared into the bottom of his empty shot glass.

The scrawny one took a large swig of his beer. "I guess you think you're pretty smart," he said to Murphy.

"Only compared to some," Murphy said.

"You hear me, stinkman?" the big guy called.

The scrawny fellow took another gulp of beer and slammed the bottle back down onto the bar. "How about compared to this?" He reached under his coat, pulled out a .357 Magnum Smith and Wesson, and pointed it at Murphy. "Who's smart now?" He fired.

The blast of the revolver knocked Murphy off his feet and backward into the counter. He landed on the floor with a *thud*. The scrawny man turned to wide-eyed Hunch, who seemed for the first time to have noticed the other customers. Another explosion, and Hunch toppled over with his bar stool.

"Man, you shot 'em both," said the big one.

"What do I always tell you? No witnesses. Quick, check the register."

But the snarling mass of grey fur and slashing claws that a second later bounded over the bar had other ideas. The big man did not check the register. He had no eyes left to see it. The scrawny one fired again, point blank into the chest of the beast—to no effect. He started to scream, but a blow from the side interrupted him. He turned to see a second monstrosity towering feet above him, hair and insane eyes, muscle and claws and teeth. Then the man looked down—and saw his intestines trailing from his open belly to the floor.

The revolver dropped from his hand. He tottered precariously, but before he could fall to his knees, the black beast before him snapped its fangs around his entrails and yanked. Several more feet of intestine spooled out onto the floor. As the scrawny man's eyes rolled up into his head and gravity at last claimed him, he had a final fleeting image of the beast gnawing his bowels.

Chapter 2

Kaitlin's head was in the refrigerator when she heard the first gunshot. At least she thought it was a gunshot; she'd spent enough time in the inner city for that sound in the night not to be a stranger. It sounded enough like a gunshot that the second one, a few seconds later, made her bang her head on the underside of the top shelf. The top shelf was the only shelf in the refrigerator; the middle one had broken long ago, so now there were two large square spaces, mostly full of leftovers in varying stages of what Kaitlin liked to call "final reclamation," which was to say: decomposition.

The smell was not pleasant. Upon opening the refrigerator door, she had reminded herself that she needed to clean out the whole thing, as she had similarly reminded herself every time she opened the door for the past several months. The shelves on the refrigerator door were packed with cans of cheap beer. Kaitlin did not drink beer or alcohol of any type; the shelves were a monument to her two years of sobriety. Sobriety and solitude. She had never really *wanted* to drink, and it was mostly other people who had kindled her *need* to drink. Isolation had seemed the best solution.

The third gunshot, short on the heels of the second, was definitely a gunshot. The sound was not quite so frightening out here in the wilderness as it always had been in the city. Here, people hunted. Occasionally a hunter shot another hunter, or a stray bullet went through somebody's kitchen window, but at least there was the underlying assumption that, unlike in the city, people did not intentionally shoot at other people. Kaitlin had broken herself of her city reflexes: to drop to the floor at the sound of gunfire. After all, by the time you heard a shot, it was too late; if that bullet was going to get you, it would have gotten you. But often there were more than one, and dropping to the floor at the first sound could save you from the ensuing crossfire. With so much forested acreage in this region, gunfire from hunters was part of the scenery.

But usually it wasn't multiple shots in rapid succession so nearby. And usually it wasn't in the middle of the night.

Kaitlin dropped to the floor. In the process, she spilled what might have been the only mostly-edible leftover in her refrigerator, a bowl of several-days-old macaroni and cheese.

She stayed low against the cold linoleum. The old, rickety, frame house was not well insulated—thus she had been able to afford it. She was accustomed to wearing a threadbare wool sweater, long johns, jeans, boots, and a blanket over her shoulders, all just to keep warm, but the linoleum sucked the heat from her tiny body. After a few minutes, hearing no more gunfire, she used her fingers to scoop the macaroni and cheese back into the bowl and returned it to the refrigerator. Munchies could wait. Not having been shot, her imprudent curiosity was now piqued.

Kaitlin was not oblivious to the fact that throughout her twenty-three years of life, many focuses of her curiosity had been ill-advised: alcohol, drugs, sex, men in general, fundamentalist Christianity, fundamentalist Islam, Scientology, the Democratic party, the Republican party, small-d democracy, socialism, rap music... But no matter how dramatic the particular debacle, and they were as varied as they were numerous, no matter in what way she came away disillusioned and dispirited from the panacea of the month, she had always found, often to her surprise, that one aspect of her personality rebounded in full: her curiosity, her desire to seek out answers, her need to *know*.

It was that perverse need to know that now would not allow her merely to peer out the kitchen window, down the road toward the ramshackle bar, where she guessed the shots had come from. She considered — for almost a split second — calling the police. In her old neighborhood, the cops weren't necessarily the answer to every problem; depending on which officer showed up on the doorstep, they might *be* the problem. And Kaitlin didn't have a lot of confidence in the good-ole-boy sheriffs out here in the sticks either. There weren't a whole lot of people of color, of mixed parentage, this far from the urban centers. Kaitlin had the feeling that every law enforcement officer that came within a mile of her thought that she was a prostitute, a runaway, a crack addict, if not all three. It didn't help that her stash of pot upstairs made her a little sensitive to official scrutiny, perhaps even defensive. But there it was. The cops were right out.

She turned off the kitchen light so her eyes could adjust to the darkness and she could see farther outside. The light from the run-down bar, Murphy's Something-or-Another, burned dimly not quite a quarter mile away. She could see the stupid beer sign blinking in the window. That had bothered her when she first moved in — on, off, on, off, on, off — but now it was nothing more than a satellite pulsing far away, or even comforting like lightning bugs in the summer. Usually the bar was quiet; usually it wasn't open, and even when it was there often weren't any customers to make noise. The parking lot was just out of sight from Kaitlin's kitchen window, so she stepped out onto the porch. From there, she didn't see any cars, not even the old Pacer that she thought must belong to the owner, but there could be some parked around the side, hidden from her view by the side of the building.

She thought again about calling the cops.... But she hadn't heard any more shots—if they really were gunshots. As the sounds themselves receded further into the past, her memory grew less distinct, as did her recognition. If somebody shot somebody else, she thought, the gunman—she knew from her time in the city that the shooter was almost always a man—was probably long gone. The victim might not be so lucky. He or she might need help. But they probably weren't gunshots at all. Still...

Telling herself that she was only going part way—just to see and listen for any more commotion—Kaitlin made her way off the porch, through the front yard, and along the road. In her mind, the fact that she still had the blanket wrapped around her shoulders, that she hadn't put on her parka, reinforced her assertion that she just wanted a peek. She was sure that this was not one of those instances where she gave in to denial and self-delusion and ended up where she shouldn't. She'd been down *that* road too many times before.

She'd just take a peek.

A sheen of frost coated the asphalt, and the clomp of Kaitlin's boots seemed to her to reverberate through the trees, so she kept to the grassy shoulder. Even the crunchy, frost-encrusted grass sounded loud, but there was no other good option. If she moved farther into the woods, she'd have trouble seeing in the dark, and dead leaves would crackle underfoot. The moon shining through the break in the canopy over the road gave her enough light in the open space; she just had to step very slowly to minimize the crunching, and to be careful of the rusted beer cans and other litter strewn beside the road.

Almost before she realized it, Kaitlin was farther than she'd meant to go. She looked back and forth from the bar to her house, and the bar was the closer of the two buildings. But she still could see only a portion of the parking lot. No cars. Unless they were parked farther around the other side, toward the back of the lot. Just a few more steps would probably be enough to tell.... The front light was on, as was the light inside. A little closer, and she might be able to see if anyone was inside; from within, they'd never see her in the dark. So she inched ahead. One careful step at a time.

That was when both the inside and outside lights at the bar went out. Kaitlin froze as she heard the door open. She was blinded by the sudden total darkness. Her heart pounded like the wings of a hummingbird. Instinctively, she crouched down, hoping not to be seen.

Growling from the direction of the bar. Somebody had dogs, hunting dogs. Let them be on leashes, Kaitlin prayed. The weight of footsteps on gravel.

But as her eyes adjusted to the new level of darkness, and the moon and stars did their work of lightening the night sky, she didn't see the shapes of dogs—but of two men, each carrying something slung over his shoulder.

Kaitlin held her breath. The hair on the back of her neck was standing straight up. She suddenly had to make a concerted effort not to pee her pants. Something was not right about the two men. Kaitlin fought the urge to scream, to run back to the house, lock the doors and huddle in the farthest corner of the basement. The men would definitely see her if she did that, but the impulse was powerful, if not rational. Sudden terror twisted her belly, and cold sweat ran down the small of her back, and from her armpits down her sides. She was shivering, not from the cold; she clenched her teeth together to keep them quiet.

Her lungs began to burn. She forced herself to exhale, and this sound seemed as loud as air escaping a punctured tire. She couldn't get a deep breath; she hiccuped in a mouthful of cold air that seared her throat. Beginning to panic, she clamped a hand over her mouth—muffled the sound of her panting, warmed the air she couldn't help but gasp in.

From across the road at the bar, she saw eyes. Scanning the darkness. Looking for her. One of the men was out of sight, around the building. But the other was looking for her. Then she realized what was not right about the men. Size. They were out of proportion. They were way too tall to have fit through the door of the bar upright. And the sacks slung over their shoulders... As the one peering into the darkness shifted his position, Kaitlin thought she saw part of the shape over his shoulder more clearly. A foot—a limp foot at the end of a limp, dangling leg.

She pressed her hand more tightly over her mouth. She panted through her nose, and began to see spots. She was dizzy. Mustn't hyperventilate, pass out.

Now the eyes saw her. The animal gaze swept past her. Came back to rest on her. Again the urge to flee, to scream. Had to breathe. Hell with peeing on herself.

She flinched at a loud, dull noise. Something dropped against metal. Into the back of a pickup truck. The man—the *thing*—stared at her for a moment longer...then turned away, loped around the side of the building. It was so quick, its movements so fluid, graceful, powerful. It was there with its burden, and then it was gone.

This time, Kaitlin didn't hesitate. She turned and ran. She wasn't sure over the noise of her breathing and her furiously pounding heart and her boots crunching frozen grass if she heard a second dull thud against metal, and she didn't care. She didn't look back when an engine turned over, and she was racing through the side yard to the back by the time headlights illuminated the road in front of her house.

Chapter 3

B lack Rindle did most of the digging. The hump on his back was greatly exaggerated in his rage-form, his massive man-wolf body. He stood stooped and walked with a limp; it seemed appropriate that he should dig in the dirt.

"You dig the holes, Hunch," Ryan EveSong Murphy had told him. "I'll get everything else ready."

Everything else was preparing the bodies and taking the truck elsewhere. EveSong stripped the bodies; he dug out all the teeth and bit off the fingers. The clothes and extraneous bits they would burn, the teeth scatter in the forest. The truck was a simpler matter. Evesong drove it to a bluff a few miles distant and then let the pickup roll off, down an embankment, and into the pond below. Some hunter or hiker would find it eventually. Big deal.

By the time Evesong returned on foot, Black Rindle had dug the hole, dragged the big faceless man and the smaller disemboweled one into it, and then covered them over with dirt and leaves and sticks. He urinated on the grave for good measure. He felt certain that either of the two dead men would have done the same for him were their situations reversed.

EveSong sniffed the wet leaves then added his own scent. "Some humans just beg to be killed," he said.

Black Rindle grunted. Leave it to EveSong to need the final word, to ruminate about what required no further discussion.

The men had chosen the wrong place to rob. They were dead. End of story, as far as Black Rindle was concerned.

"You sure took your time gutting the one that had the gun," EveSong said, not yet having talked the subject into the ground fully enough to satisfy him. "One would think that you *wanted* him to shoot me again."

"Didn't know you were so fragile," Black Rindle muttered.

"You truly are a blight upon our people."

"If you didn't want to get shot, you should have killed the one with gun first."

"I thought I would have help—*timely* help, that is."

Black Rindle just grunted. EveSong's excuse was a load of crap. He'd been angry, and the big guy had been closer. That's all there was to it. But there was no sense in arguing, not with EveSong.

"That's it," EveSong said. "I don't want to see you in my bar again. Ever. You drink too much, and you're no good to anybody. Your own dam is laid low, near death, all because of you. You rotted her from the inside out. Gaia is punishing her for inflicting you upon us."

Black Rindle flinched. What could he say? His mother, Galia Rainchild, *was* on death's door. And everyone knew that he *was* the accursed of Gaia. His misshapen body was proof of that. And as for being kicked out of the Tap House, this was at least the hundredth time that EveSong had banished him. Forever.

"What's that?" EveSong asked, pointing to a blanket slung over a tree branch.

"A blanket."

"I can see that. Where'd you get it?"

"Found it."

EveSong tossed his hands up, disgusted by the unhelpful answer. "A blight upon our people," he said, shaking his head.

Black Rindle didn't see that it was any of EveSong's business. Black Rindle was the one who'd found the blanket; he was the one who'd seen the woman by the road. If EveSong had been too busy with the bodies and the truck, that was his problem. Black Rindle had seen the woman and then followed the truck on foot. That was why he'd found the blanket. It smelled like the woman—the woman who hadn't run away, when humans always ran away.

"Evert won't be pleased by your recalcitrance, Hunch," EveSong said.

Black Rindle grunted. Evert Cloudkill was never pleased with him. No matter what. Why should this time be any different? Black Rindle took the blanket from the branch and draped it over his shoulder. As the first rays of the sun made their way over the horizon, the two Garou started their walk back to the caern.

Chapter 4

At some point after sunrise, Kaitlin decided that whatever she had seen in front of the bar was not going to storm into her house and kill her. She was crouched in the back corner of her basement, had been for hours. She'd spent the time thinking about what she'd seen, thinking about her own response, waiting for the creature to come kill her. She was cold and dirty. The basement had an earthen floor and cracked cement walls. Her legs and back were stiff, cramped from squatting for so long. Her jeans, too, were cold and stiff, wet against her legs. She reeked of urine.

There were two windows in the basement, small and near the ceiling. They were at ground level from the outside. She had not turned on the light when she'd fled to the basement; the naked bulb hanging by a wire would have seemed like a beacon, calling beasts to violate and destroy her. Instead, she'd huddled in dark terror until gradually the two pathetic windows had grown brighter. Dawn had intruded hesitantly in the basement, almost as hesitantly as Kaitlin had left her hiding place.

She felt a little better once she climbed up the stairs to the back hallway. She hardly noticed the basement grime that her boots tracked on the once-white linoleum in the kitchen. She was too relieved to see, to stand in, the full light of morning; she'd doubted that she would ever see another, and as she stood on her dingy, grime-covered linoleum, the grey, overcast daybreak was as spectacular as any she'd ever experienced.

Her house was not warm; it was drafty, and the windows rattled in strong winds. But it received a generous amount of light; that and the price were what had convinced her to buy it. The windows were large, with the old wavy glass that made things outside ripple if you moved while looking through. By design or by accident, the windows were situated to take full advantage of what little light there was during the long Michigan winter. Morning enlivened the kitchen. Afternoon illuminated the dining room—what was *supposed* to be the dining room. Kaitlin never ate there; she ate in the kitchen at the card table with the cold, folding, metal chair. The dining room was full of bottles and cans that she meant to haul to the recycling center some day—except Kaitlin didn't have a car, so some day, like tomorrow, never came. So the boxes and crates filled up, one after another, and then were stacked one atop another; each week less of the scratched, hardwood floor was visible. The house was large enough that she had quite a while still before a trip to the recycling center became urgent.

The evening sun, when the shadows grew long and the light, for a few brief moments made the world look like it wasn't a complete and utter hellhole, shone in the front parlor, which Kaitlin never used, and into her bedroom upstairs. She would sit in bed under her fraying quilt, and maybe read, or smoke a joint, as outside the colors of the world eased from red and orange to yellow and brown to purple and grey and finally black.

Aside from the card table and the folding chair in the kitchen, Kaitlin's bed was the only other piece of furniture in the house.

This morning after her hours of solitary confinement in the basement, Kaitlin took special note of her bright and (at least by comparison to the basement) shiny kitchen. Besides being stiff and cold and wet, she was hungry. She took the macaroni and cheese from the refrigerator, spooned the moldy portion into the sink, and took the rest with her upstairs, shoveling it into her mouth as she went.

She set food aside as she peeled off her jeans and underwear and threw them in the claw-footed iron tub. After washing herself from the waist down, she put on fresh underwear and set to washing by hand her only pair of jeans. Wringing the heavy, wet denim was hard work, but it was the drying that threatened to drive her crazy. Half naked, she scurried out onto the upstairs porch and hung her pants over the railing so they could catch the breeze, then she scurried back inside and retreated under her quilt. Sitting, Kaitlin pulled her knees up against her chest, with only her head and hands poking out from beneath the quilt so she could roll a joint on top of her knees. She didn't relish the prospect of putting on the jeans, even when they were dry; they'd be cold and stiff, but the dryer, like the washing machine, was broken, so there was no way around it. Maybe, she thought, she'd stick them in the bed with her for a while to warm them up before she put them on.

Now that the immediate necessities were taken care of — washing, food, joint — Kaitlin's hands began to tremble. And then her entire body. She drew in a deep breath and let the coarse smoke tickle her throat and lungs; she held the breath, exhaled slowly and evenly many seconds later. Her next several breaths were of cold, crisp air — her bedroom wouldn't warm appreciably until later in the day. She tried to concentrate on nothing but breathing: full, deep breaths in; long, steady, cleansing breaths out. When that seemed to be going well and the trembling had receded, she took another hit.

Feeling again relatively composed, she forced herself at last to confront what she'd seen last night: It wasn't human. That much she knew. Her observations confirmed her belief — the creature's size, its preternatural quickness and powerful bearing, its eyes glaring out into darkness—but her knowledge came from a deeper sense. A sense she had hoped to leave behind in the city, where the dead walked among the living, sometimes *within* the living, and no one seemed the wiser.

Kaitlin shuddered. She stretched her neck forward, like a turtle poking its head out of a quilted shell, and put her lips to the joint again. Isolation, simplicity—they had allowed her to restore a semblance of control and stability to her life. But now the unwanted vision had found her out. If only she hadn't heard the gunshots last night…if only she had *stayed in the house*…if only that creature, that thing, hadn't seen her…if only…

It was carrying a body, she reminded herself—though she would have liked to have forgotten that fact. It had killed someone. These monsters that she saw, sometimes they seemed harmless; sometimes they killed people. Kaitlin laughed; she choked and blew smoke out into the room. Didn't seem an equitable flip of the coin, somehow: heads, sad lonely spirit; tails, deranged serial killer.

Even if the creature hadn't been carrying a body last night, Kaitlin's own visceral response would have told her the worst. That was the way of these episodes. She couldn't always pinpoint the details that led her to know what she knew—she *often* couldn't pinpoint the details—but the overwhelming wave of panic-terror that had seized her there in the dark by the road was a warning. Sometimes coming unexpected upon one of these supernatural denizens she felt sympathy, like for the ethereal mother and young daughter who Kaitlin had watched crossing the same street, time and again, hour after hour, day after day. Sometimes Kaitlin felt apprehension, but never before had she been so completely undone by bone-deep fear. Never before had she seen or felt anything like what she had last night, or sensed such barely restrained fury. Instinctively, her hand strayed to her throat as if to protect herself.

A warning to the wise. To the curious.

By afternoon, the wind had done its job. Kaitlin snatched her jeans from the railing and stuffed them under the quilt with her until the worst of the chill was gone. They were still a tad damp around the pockets, but having retrieved her bowl from the bathroom and finished the macaroni and cheese, she was acutely aware that there was no more food in the house, and the store was a five-mile hike. She needed to get started.

Not until she pulled on her parka did she realize that she had lost her blanket. Normally her routine for going out in the cold was take off the blanket, which was perpetually wrapped about her shoulders from late fall to early spring, and put on the parka. She'd been cold huddled in the basement, but her thoughts had been too anxious and scattered to touch on the blanket, and the rest of the morning she'd been under the quilt.

Reconstructing events of the misplacement was simple enough: She had the blanket when she left the house last night; she didn't remember having it since she returned. No big deal, she told herself. She might find it on the way to the store, or she could get another at the Salvation Army store in Winimac, if it came to that. But a disquieting sense of foreboding accompanied her realization that the blanket was missing. An unforeseen side effect of owning so little was that each particular belonging took on enormous emotional as well as practical value; the blanket was not merely a possession, it was a friend, a confidant. Simplicity, though it reduced the number of attachments, in its own perverse way intensified the nature of what attachments remained.

Perspective, Kaitlin told herself. Must keep perspective. Just a ratty, threadbare blanket.

Bundled up with her parka and a scarf, she tried to retrace her steps from last night, from the back of the house around the side to the road. As she walked, unpleasant thoughts tickled the back of her brain: She knew that in the past she had encountered...things, supernatural beings, during the day, in broad daylight, and that made the afternoon sun less comforting. The worst, she reminded herself, seemed to happen at night. The day, even overcast, *felt* safe. The open spaces, the evergreens and the bare hardwoods, they all seemed right, normal; they tried to convince Kaitlin that she hadn't seen what she thought she'd seen in the darkness. And she was more than willing to believe. It was possible.... It even seemed likely, now that the sun was up, despite the obscuring clouds. Kaitlin felt better merely contemplating the possibility that she'd been mistaken. She was pleased that she could be so reasonable.

Walking along the grassy shoulder, she didn't see her blanket. It would have been fairly obvious were it lying there. Were the bent blades of grass before her markers of her passing last night? she wondered. She scanned the woods to her right. The wind had probably blown her blanket beyond the ditch; it would be tangled among fallen branches, or snagged on a stump.

But when she reached the point she thought was the farthest she'd come last night, there was still no blanket. Could the wind have blown it *across* the road? she wondered. She retraced her steps, walked across the pavement, and followed the shoulder the same distance on that side. Nothing but litter and patches of old snow in spots the sun didn't reach.

Kaitlin sighed and her voice formed a cloud. Thwarted in her search and rescue mission, she needed to head on to the grocery store nonetheless. She'd taken fifteen dollars from the cigar box under her bed, enough to buy approximately sixty boxes of macaroni and cheese—or maybe fifty, and a little fruit to ward off scurvy.

Her first impulse was to cross back to the other side of the road, to have the pavement between herself and the bar, which she had to pass. But she felt silly, cowardly, doing that in full daylight. There was never anyone at the bar until very late in the afternoon. Nothing could happen to her just walking through the parking lot near the road.

Especially if she *had* been mistaken last night, which seemed more and more likely all the time.

Maybe somebody had merely been carrying out an empty keg hoisted on his shoulder. No, it wasn't the right shape for a keg. Maybe bags of garbage. Or even if it *was* a person, it might have just been a drunk buddy—and the eight-and-a-half-foot-tall guy with the glowing eyes and bulging muscles had just been carrying him to the truck. Maybe the whole thing had been an acid flashback.

Kaitlin took a deep breath and tried not to think about last night. She pressed onward, refusing to cross back to the other side of the road for such silly reasons.

The bar did indeed appear deserted as she approached it. The beer sign wasn't flashing; the shades on the inside of the door and windows were pulled down. The owner's Pacer was still parked behind the bar. Was he okay? she wondered. Was he in there, or was he one of the bodies carried out?

Not bodies, she corrected herself. Bags of garbage, or...or whatever.

Thoughts of the grocery store and macaroni and cheese were shoved to the back of Kaitlin's mind as curiosity bullied its way relentlessly to the fore. What was the harm of checking to see if maybe the shades weren't pulled quite all the way down? If she could just see that everything inside was all right, then...then what? She wasn't sure. It wouldn't prove that nothing had happened last night, that two huge upright beasts hadn't carried bodies out. Nothing was a problematic thing to prove. But she *was* sure that if she looked inside and there wasn't blood splattered from floor to ceiling, she would feel at least a little bit better. And wasn't peace of mind important?

That was why she'd moved out here to the boondocks in the first place, after all.

Carrying herself with more confidence than she actually felt, Kaitlin marched up to the front of Murphy's Tap House. It was a squat, cinderblock building with only two windows on the front wall and one on the door. None on the sides. Unfortunately, the shades *were* pulled all the way down. Kaitlin pressed her face against the glass and squinted around the edges of each window, but it was no use. She went so far as to try the doorknob gingerly, despite her fear that the owner might be inside, but the door was locked.

With a sigh, she laid her forehead against the window on the door, her fingers on either side of her face, like the feet of water spiders resting lightly on the surface of a muddied, opaque pond. She made the mistake of thinking again about what had happened last night — and the visions began.

She felt her knees buckle, but she was far away — far within herself, watching what she had not seen. Kaitlin had not seen, but the glass knew, and the cinderblocks knew, and as surely as every aspect of creation is of one mind and one spirit, they revealed to Kaitlin their secrets.

The shapes were familiar, large and powerful. Larger than human should be, larger than humans *could* be. And closer, angrier. A whirling blur of fur, teeth, claws. Rage. She saw two bodies also. Saw them *become* bodies, the life ripped from them in bloody shreds. Face and throat. Belly sliced open, guts spilled to the floor. She was awash in blood, lifeblood flowing away to nothing, seeping into a listless concrete floor. Lost amidst the horror was a gunshot, the third. Futile. Useless against the beast's blood-soaked, slavering grin. Then the other beast stood, human entrails trailing from its jaws. And she saw the eyes. The same eyes that she had seen last night. The same eyes that had seen her.

Kaitlin jumped away from the door. The window shattered and she screamed. The glass remained intact, but cobweb fissures covering the entire pane radiated out from ten separate points—where she had touched. Kaitlin looked at her fingertips. One was bleeding.

"Can I help you, miss?"

Kaitlin jumped again but didn't scream this time. She whirled to see a man about twenty yards away, coming toward her. He had dark hair, short and tidy like his beard, and wore a warm flannel shirt, jeans, and well-worn boots. As he came closer, the visions assailed Kaitlin once more. Her sight flashed, strobe-like, and with each step the man changed. He was himself, and then he was one of the snarling wolfish monstrosities; he was himself, and then he was giant and bloody, eyes and claws gleaming death.

"Miss?" he said again as he reached her.

Kaitlin couldn't move; if she could have, she would have run. But her legs failed her again. She staggered, just managing to take a step to steady herself. The man was looking past her, looking at the door, at the broken pain of glass.

"Someone broke your window," she said, consciously realizing what part of her mind already knew: This was the man she'd seen getting in and out of the Pacer before; the owner of the car, the owner of the bar. And he was one of the beasts.

"I can see that," he said, his voice and expression cooler than they had been at first. "You should take care of your finger," he said.

Kaitlin looked again at her bleeding index finger. The clean slice was not quite an inch long, almost to the first joint, but it bled freely. She wrapped her other hand around the finger, squeezed.

"You should keep your nose clean, too," the man said, at the same time reaching forward and actually brushing her nose with his finger which, he showed her, came away dirty.

Dumbfounded, she looked at his finger, and then back at the door. She saw her greasy noseprint on the dusty, cracked glass and understood. Kaitlin didn't look at his face. She tried not to blink; if she blinked, he might become the monster she had seen. If she didn't meet his gaze, he wouldn't rip her face off with razor claws. She couldn't speak; her mouth was suddenly as dry as if she'd swallowed a handful of gravel dust from the parking lot. She stared at her own white knuckles, stained red by the droplets of blood seeping out between her fingers.

"I..." Her tongue was parched—thick and useless. Staring at the ground, she saw pools of blood around the man's shoes. Now she did blink, holding her eyes tightly shut for a moment, and the blood was gone.

"Let me see that." He gripped her wrist, pulled her to him, strong but not rough, until she opened her hand and showed him the finger. "I don't think you need stitches, or a doctor. Do you need a ride somewhere?"

The thought horrified Kaitlin. She couldn't fathom getting into his car any more than she could walking into his blood-drenched bar. "I... No. I live..." She started to turn and point back to her house, which was just visible from where they stood, but then realized that the last thing she wanted to tell this man was where she lived.

He watched her expectantly, looking back and forth between her face and her wavering finger. "You live...that way?"

She followed his gaze, stared at her own finger as if it were a disembodied head, or a bird of prey about to pounce on her, and she very deliberately pulled it back to her body. "Not far," she stammered.

He nodded as if he understood, but his expression bellied that point. "Well, if you're sure. You look awfully pale."

"I'm...fine."

"If you say so. It's just a little blood, you know. You must not be a hunter. Hunting gets you used to blood."

"Thank you," Kaitlin said, though she wasn't sure what she was thanking him for. Maybe for not ripping her face off, or strewing her entrails amidst the gravel. She turned away from him and began walking numbly back home. She listened for his footsteps, either pursuing her or retreating to the bar, but he must have stood and watched her for quite a while.

Kaitlin thought absently of macaroni and cheese, but she couldn't make herself care about food. She wondered if she would ever be hungry again after what she had seen. She didn't think so.

Chapter 5

B lack Rindle awoke to pain. He had not meant to fall asleep—not here leaning against the wall of the cave as he watched over Galia. Balthazar was awake; *he* watched over Galia faithfully, though he bore no ties of blood to her. *He* watched her chest rise and fall with faltering breath, and her paws twitch and pad at the ground. Perhaps she hunted in her dreams. Never had she spoken to Balthazar—he had arrived at the caern after she had taken ill—yet he was her unwavering guardian, sitting cross-legged beside her night and day—while Black Rindle slept.

A stiff neck pained Black Rindle as he awoke to the fading light, but the crick was soothing compared to the loathing he felt for his own weakness, his own faithlessness. He was accustomed to pain; his man-form was never free of it, except when eased by alcohol, and the guilt of the accursed was never far from his heart, no matter the shape of his body.

"Does she speak?" Black Rindle asked.

Balthazar Spirit-Walker slowly turned his head to face the intruder, to take him in with the hard gaze of a magistrate looking upon the guilty. "Her spirit grows weaker. She does not wake. She does not speak." The Strider, amazingly, maintained his vigil as Crinos, but his man-wolf form revealed outwardly none of the rage that must surely fuel him. Black Rindle marveled at such stoic restraint, though he suspected that Balthazar's disdainful regard for all other members of the sept was a chink in the watcher's armor of control. Perhaps behind that façade of superiority a torrent of pressure grew ever more intense, until one day it must burst forth. Or perhaps Spirit-Walker was simply a better Garou, stronger of will, more dedicated and persistent, and his contempt of the others was fairly won. Especially his contempt of Black Rindle.

Balthazar kept a small fire to warm Galia; the smoke, in the enclosed space, burned Black Rindle's eyes and throat. The cave was little more than a hollow space beneath a large rock, but it served to protect Black Rindle's dam from the elements.

"Has Evert been by?" Black Rindle asked.

"He comes most days, but will not stay. He will not come at all while you are here." Balthazar's flat words conveyed what the watcher did not say outright: *The fault here is yours, Black Rindle. And Evert Cloudkill is little better than you.*

Black Rindle would have taken offense, would have surrendered himself to rage, had the unspoken accusations not been true. Galia Rainchild grew weaker with every day that passed, and the caern, too. Many of the Garou could not see — but those who did, knew where the fault lay. Black Rindle knew. Balthazar Spirit-Walker knew. Yet the knowledge went unspoken. Evert Cloudkill knew — yet he did nothing.

Stirring from his place of accidental slumber, Black Rindle crawled toward Galia. He looked upon her restless sleep and wished that he could take her pain and fever upon himself. If only he could die in her place... Birthing him years ago was her only injudicious act, the only sin for which she might conceivably be punished. It would have been better for them all had she devoured the pup when it crawled deformed from her womb, yet she had suffered it to live. In giving life to the accursed, she had taken his taint upon herself; with time she had rotted, and soon she would die.

Black Rindle reached out and laid his hands on the side of her lupine body; he traced the lay of her fur grown thin. And for a moment, her restlessness seemed to leave her. Her paws lay limp, and she breathed deeply, as if sighing in her sleep. He looked up at Balthazar, but could find no hint of mercy in the Strider's gaze, no suggestion that Black Rindle's touch might have eased her pain. He drew back his hands, fearing that he had harmed her, that the deep breath she drew would be her last. Of what crimes would the others accuse him, her miscreant child, then?

He dared one last touch, brushing his fingers against her ear, before he crawled away from her, out from beneath the sheltering rock. He did not look back; what need did he have to meet Balthazar's uncompromising glare?

Beyond the cave and the trickle of smoke meandering listlessly heavenward, the caern was still, quiet, lifeless. The stream, almost dry, thirsted for the spring thaw. Birch and maple, stark and winter-stripped, swayed at the mercy of the cold westerly wind. The veil of color provided by the white pines seemed worn. Black Rindle could not escape the malaise that hovered over the Sept of the Wailing Glade; the forest itself seemed muted, tired. How could the other Garou not to see it? Were they unable or unwilling? Evert Cloudkill, as Alpha and Theurge, should know, but surely he would have warned the rest of them. Balthazar, too, was Theurge, but since arriving at the sept he had only ever paid notice to Galia, she who was also of the crescent moon. Galia *would* have know; she would have warned the sept—if she weren't dying. But she seemed to share the affliction. For many weeks, she had not communicated with anyone, had not so much as shifted from her wolf-form. And all the while, Evert said nothing. If the Theurges, the spirit-voices of the people, did not speak, then how could Black Rindle, accursed among Garou and deformed, hope to warn the sept? He could not hope. He had none.

The cloud-thick smothering sky weighed down upon Black Rindle as much as did the silence, as did the sickness of the land.

The caern to him seemed a skeleton of its former self, flesh rotted away, marrow dried. Or perhaps, he thought, the sickness was merely within him. Perhaps a few drinks would wash clean the pallor of decay from the rest of the world. EveSong might be at his bar at this hour; there was blood to be scrubbed. Exiled or not, Black Rindle's help would probably be welcomed, and he'd just as soon not see the other members of the sept tonight—or any night. The hunting pack was probably abroad in the forest. Evert Cloudkill was no doubt off brooding. That left very few Garou unaccounted for, one of whom, much to Black Rindle's chagrin, came loping up to him now.

"Have you heard?" Barks-at-Shadows asked expectantly, excitedly. "A tale-telling tonight. A fire and fresh venison and EveSong will tell stories."

Black Rindle did not pause, did not acknowledge the other's presence. Barks-at-Shadows was one of the few whom Black Rindle could slight with impunity—if no one else was around. Other members of the sept treated even the moon-calf, the disfavored Fang, with more respect than they accorded Black Rindle.

"A tale-telling!" Barks-at-Shadows said again, following along. "EveSong will favor us with stories and song!" In his man-form, Barks-at-Shadows' eyes did not appear to focus on quite the same spot; he held his head slightly askew, always.

"EveSong likes nothing more than to hear his own voice," Black Rindle growled. "Had he not been born Galliard, he would have crawled back into his mother and waited until Luna Gibbous came around again."

Barks-at-Shadows' puppyish enthusiasm drained away to slack-jawed confusion. "But the stories...they are our past. Without them we are little better than humans."

"You are little better than human as it is," Black Rindle said. "Maybe worse."

Not the swiftest of Garou, still Barks-at-Shadows knew the sound of name-calling. "*You* should have been of Luna Gibbous, all swollen and hump-backed."

"*Hunch*," EveSong said, appearing suddenly from the deepening darkness of the forest. "We call him *Hunch*, moon-calf. If you say *hump*, you may find him on your leg."

Barks-at-Shadows laughed, more nervous than understanding. He didn't like bickering, but he seemed always to forget how surly Black Rindle was. As for Ryan EveSong, Barks-at-Shadows *knew* that he was clever, and laughed at almost anything the Galliard said.

Black Rindle left the two of them. Perhaps, he thought, he would go break into EveSong's bar and steal liquor. That would show the pompous windbag. Worse than the taunts, which Black Rindle had suffered from his earliest days, was the fact that the sept valued the idiot moon-calf more than him. The Fang, sent away from his own petulant, inbred people, rejected by his own—but not so completely as Black Rindle was rejected by his own.

A tale telling. That prospect did little to cheer Black Rindle. There were no heroic stories, no triumphant songs, about the accursed of Gaia—or if there were, EveSong did not share them. Always the deformed metis was the idiot, the Wyrm-tainted, the villain. Bone Gnawers and stupid humans fared well in some of the stories, but never one like Black Rindle. But at least there would be food around the fire. And maybe drink.

When he came to the place where he had left his new blanket hanging on a tree, Black Rindle was not pleased to see another septmate pawing at it on the ground.

"It is *mine*," Black Rindle snarled at Claudia Stands Firm.

The wolf turned to face him and bared her teeth. Before he reached her, she changed to her natural woman-form, smaller than Black Rindle but strong and sure. "Do you speak to me in that tone, Hunch?" she glowered.

Black Rindle cast his gaze downward. The Warder *would* have sniffed out anything new to the caern; she would have noticed his scent on the blanket as well, but to investigate was her nature, her duty. "It is mine," he said again, more meekly, and snatched up the blanket. He sniffed it. The smell of the human woman was still strongly in evidence.

"Watch yourself, Hunch," she said, "or did I hear by your voice that you're ready to challenge me?" Her hand rested on the hilt of the klaive at her belt. Black Rindle still did not meet her eyes; his silence was answer enough. "I thought not."

Black Rindle wrapped the blanket into a ball and clutched it to his chest as he limped away from Stands Firm.

Chapter 6

Sparks and dancing embers lurched skyward in bacchanalian spasms, urged to frenzy by fiery brands shifting and grease dripping into the flames from venison run through on a spit. Not all the Garou took their meat cooked. The hunters in particular drew their sustenance from raw, bloody flesh. Shreds Birch held a foreleg bone between her paws and worked at a stringy tendon with her fierce jaws. Cynthia Slack Ear gnawed meat from a rib she'd snapped from the deer's carcass. Frederich Night Terror crunched meat and bone alike.

From the shadows nearby, beyond the light and warmth of crackling flames, Black Rindle busied himself with a gristly slab that Stands Firm had tossed his way. He tried not to watch the others; their rough play and dancing and howling set his teeth on edge with cold envy. But his eyes were constantly drawn back to his septmates, come from different places and different tribes to this place—this place of his blood and his birth. Yet he was the outcast, his deformity an outward sign of his inner stain and the forbidden union that had created him.

He looked at Evert Cloudkill, sitting among the festive chaos, yet aloof, brooding still. The Alpha gnawed absently, joylessly, at his food. Black Rindle looked toward the cave, but he could not see Galia, or mysterious Balthazar, or even the faint glow of the hearthfire. Black Rindle watched the others eating and play-fighting around the fire. He saw Barks-at-Shadows holding a small white orb to the firelight, gazing into the eyeball, perhaps searching for the departed spirit of the deer.

They were Black Rindle's sept, but he could summon nothing but resentment and loathing for them—the same sentiments they accorded him.

Then, to his surprise, Stands Firm moved to the edge of the gathering, near Black Rindle. She held in her hand an earthenware jug, and offered it to him.

The first jug of whiskey, which earlier Night Terror had tossed his way, had been empty. Black Rindle's spirits had risen momentarily as he'd reached up to catch it, then feeling its hollow weight and hearing the mocking laughter of the others, he berated himself for thinking that they would include him in their feast any more than necessary. So it was that now he stared distrustfully at the proffered jug, at Stands Firm. She was a harsh woman, but not cruel like some of the others. Still, Black Rindle studied her for sign of betrayal or, worse, of pity.

While Black Rindle mulled her intentions, EveSong swept past and plucked the jug from her hand. "No need to waste fine drink on Hunch," he said cheerfully. "As much time as he passes consorting with spirits, you'd think he was born of the crescent moon."

Black Rindle snarled and pulled deeper into the shadows. Let them mock, he thought. But let them dare not forget that he was Ahroun, warrior born.

EveSong had not so much forgotten as almost instantly put Black Rindle out of mind. The Galliard returned to the center of the gathering, and as he upended the jug and took a deep draught, a hush fell over the assemblage. The teller of tales was ready to regale them.

"Listen to any rock, to the wind blowing through the leaves of any tree, and you will have a story to tell," EveSong began, disinterestedly picking his teeth with the point snapped from an antler. "Each pine needle that drops to the ground came from somewhere. Each acorn is from a mighty oak that was once no more than an acorn itself. Each honking goose has seen from high above the trees what only the clouds and spirits see. Could we but hear and learn all of the different stories, we would know the past, understand the present, and see the way of the future. Some say that Gaia herself is the collected, living wisdom of all stories bound together, and that we the Garou should call ourselves Gaia's storytellers rather than Gaia's warriors."

Frederich Night Terror rewarded that speculation with an ominous growl.

EveSong shrugged noncommittally and tossed the antler point onto the fire. "Me—I but tell the stories and leave the weightier matters of philosophy and religion to the crescent moons. Which brings me to our story tonight...."

His pause drew out, encompassing them all, even Black Rindle, until it seemed the story was to be the crackling of the fire and the dance of the embers. In the darkness, Owl hooted his blessing that the bard should proceed.

"Some few weeks back, Barks-at-Shadows asked me how it was that the Sept of the Wailing Glade came to have its name," EveSong said. Barks-at-Shadows fidgeted with anticipation, so pleased was he to be mentioned in a story told before the sept. "Now, with any question, there is a short answer—but like a single pebble trying to dam a river, the short answer can never touch more than a few mere droplets of the truth. So, with your indulgence, I will endeavor to place pebble upon pebble upon pebble, until like determined Beaver we see all the raging river spread out before us, calm enough to show us the way into the land beyond.

"Now, the story of a place is often the story of people, and so is the case tonight. For to do justice to *this* place, we must needs begin in another place, far to the south and the east. A cub there was, not long past his first change. He knew enough to see that the world he'd grown up in, the world of the humans, was no world at all: blind to the spirits, deaf to the cries of Gaia. But the ways of the Garou were new and strange to him as well. So he retreated from both the old and the new. He climbed to the top of a mountain, where he could sit in the light of Mother Gaia and watch for answers in the stars. He looked inward, as well. Within himself he saw a great light, but also darkness.

"The light was his heart, the glimmering of the true Way that had been hidden from him for so long. The darkness was his lungs, the diseased life he had breathed up to that point, not so central as his heart but surrounding it.

"There on that mountain, the cub took his claws and plucked out his own lungs, casting the darkness from him. But his passage into light was not to be so easy. Where his lungs landed on the ground, they bled black blood, and the blood took shape and form. Crude mockeries of the cub rose from the dirt, Black Spiral Dancers that were as perverted and insane as the cub was virtuous. They set upon him, and a great battle was undertaken.

"From the lower places around the mountain, the Garou who had shepherded the cub to that point looked on in wonder. A dense cloud obscured the top of the mountain—not a cloud from the heavens come down, but a cloud of churning and swirling dust raised by the struggle of the cub and the Dancers. Some desired to go aid the pup, but a test of the heart is a solitary journey, and so they stayed put and watched.

"When the cloud finally settled, the mountain top was empty, and the Garou feared that the cub was lost. But shortly thereafter, he appeared from the wooded path at the bottom of the mountain. In either fist, he gripped a black pelt, each dripping hatred and poison, leaving steaming holes where their substance touched the ground. And when they had dripped their last, nothing remained. The hatred and poison had consumed themselves. And the cub was purified.

"The Garou around that mountain praised the cub — though truly he was cub no more. Where before they had known him as Evert, now they named him Evert Cloudkill, after the battle that had raged atop the mountain and the powerful enemies he had slain."

EveSong paused to sip from his jug. The eyes of other Garou glanced furtively at Cloudkill, who for his part seemed intent only upon the glowing embers of the fire. Black Rindle, too, watched the renowned leader of the sept. Cloudkill's deep green eyes shone in the firelight. He appeared as impassive as the mountain from the tale, his care-worn wrinkles carved by streams, his stony countenance implacable, unmoving, merciless.

"The Garou hoped that Cloudkill would remain with them," EveSong, refreshed, continued. "But he was young in those days, and having come of age beneath the stars, the wanderlust seized him, perhaps filling the space he had carved from his own breast.

"Ah, but the stories I could tell of his wandering. Like the birds that Mother Gaia will soon lead back north, Cloudkill followed the path of his heart, ever with one eye toward the heavens. He journeyed west until the land meets the sea. He traveled south, over mesa and mountain, through jungle and river, until he stood at the barren tip of the world. He learned the ways of the Garou, sought out the secrets of the spirits, and fought the Wyrm wherever he crossed its path. Many vicious battles did he fight, and countless scars of body and soul does he bear for his faithfulness.

"With time, though, the wanderlust, like the flower of youth, began to wilt within his breast. In the same way that Cloudkill recognized the darkness within him, he now recognized an emptiness around his heart that would not let him rest. Where the darkness and then the wanderlust had been, there was nothing, and the ache of oblivion was far more painful than the blow of any Wyrm-beast. Though wandering no longer eased his spirit, Cloudkill wandered still, for how else was he to find what it was that might fill the void around his heart?

"He looked to the stars for guidance, but the omens of the heavens did not answer his question. He sought spirits of wisdom, yet they no longer revealed their secrets. He consulted the elders of the tribes, but the Garou were distrustful of those who were not their blood kin. The Fangs had no time for him. The Shadow Lords did naught but try to deceive him. The Get could not pause from their battle, and the Furies were too angry to listen. The Glass Walkers and Bone Gnawers were encrusted in their scabs. The Red Talons, ever direct, told him to saw off his feet and walk on all fours. The Wendigo chased the *Wasichu* away, the Fianna didn't hear him over their own singing...." EveSong paused with mock indignation at the smattering of laughter from the assemblage. "And the Children...well, it was spring, and they were busy in pursuit of their Kinfolk." EveSong grabbed his crotch and tugged, to the renewed amusement of the crowd.

"Not until the last did he journey into the land of the Uktena. Could it be, he wondered, that what he sought was buried in the earth? If so, the diggers in the dirt, the buriers of rocks and miners of lore, would know. But the Uktena were hoarders of secrets. They sent Cloudkill away. They would not talk to him—all but one. A young woman among them and not yet hard as the scorched earth, she followed after Cloudkill. She was unusual for her kind, born beneath the rare desert rain, and they named her Galia Rainchild."

The gathering around the fire fell silent at the mention of her name. In the shadows, Black Rindle felt the emptiness around his own heart; he knew that of which EveSong spoke.

"She said to Cloudkill that she knew what it was he lacked: a companion to fulfill his spirit, a soulmate to make him whole. She said that she had seen these things in a basin of spirit tears, and that his path was hers, that they should walk forward from that point as one. And so they did."

Black Rindle felt his eyes brimming with tears. He repressed a growl from the bottom of his throat; he wanted to leap from his place of seclusion and tear open EveSong's throat so that the story would end there. It would be much better for them all if it ended there. But EveSong could never let well enough alone.

"From that day forward," the Galliard continued, "the two were as one. For many years they traveled, never one without the other, and together they unlocked secrets of the spirit world that would have remained hidden from one of them alone, for Rainchild, too, was born of the crescent moon. As one they sought out wisdom, and as one they nurtured Gaia, each other, and other Garou they met. The tales of their travels are myriad, but what concerns us is that eventually, their search for wisdom brought them here.

"In those days this land was awash in humans, cutting the trees and dragging them away, boring into the earth, using hammer and explosive to tear apart the world so that they might carve out the rocks that struck their fancy. The Garou here at the time did not watch idly: They fell on bands of loggers and turned their saws against them; they tossed the miners into their holes and piled the rocks back on top of them. But always there were more humans. More to take the place of the fallen. More to cut and carve and pick and destroy.

"It was Cloudkill and Rainchild that enlisted the aid of wise Owl, and it was Owl who showed them the ways of the forest, ways to *hide* places so no humans would come near. Wherever the Garou were able, they set spirit wards in the land and in the streams. It was slow going, and not easy, but soon Owl's teachings proved true, and the humans began to pass by some of the wild places. They sought their minerals elsewhere; they turned to trees in other places, corrupted places without spirit protectors. But these lands remained green.

"There it ends, you might think, but, ah, I have yet to answer Barks-at-Shadows' question: How did we come to be called the Sept of the Wailing Glade?

"Well, once the worst of the humans forsook this place, the Garou came to realize that more than merely the droning march of humankind was at work in the land. Without the mask of human loggers and miners, the corruption in the land became evident. Spring came, but the trees did not bud. The sun shone in the sky, but snow did not melt. The deer grew thin; the bear remained in their caves.

"Owl it was who revealed to the Garou the source of the blight in their midst: a foul Bane buried far beneath the ground, birthed and grown to obscene maturity within one of the intrusive mines left behind by the humans. The Garou rose up against this menace, and many died in those dank places beneath the earth.

"Finally, it was Rainchild who entreated a serpent-spirit of Uktena's brood to aid the Garou in their battle. Water Snake came wriggling, as did many of his brothers and sisters, too many to count. They slipped down into the dark places, they overwhelmed the Bane and dragged it screaming into the light. They kept dragging it, away from its festering lair, away from the places the humans had damaged. Water Snake and his brothers and sisters dragged the Bane here, to this glade, and at the side of our stream where Rainchild had interceded on behalf of the Garou, the spirits set on the Bane in earnest.

"They struck so relentlessly and mercilessly that their swarm set the wind to blowing through the trees. Their fangs opened grievous wounds on the demon and its corrupting blood dripped steaming to the ground. As the sun dipped below the horizon and Sister Luna rose in the sky, Water Snake and his brood churned the stream into a roiling torrent, and then the stream itself rose, a mighty serpent poised to strike and cleanse the land.

"Over the noise of the tumult, a new sound made itself heard: a moan of cowardice and terror, a rising mournful dirge as the Bane looked upon its own doom and knew the fear and despair that so long it had spawned. The sound grew to a deafening peak, an ear-splitting piteous wail, as the spirit of the stream and the Garou together struck one final blow and tore the Bane asunder!" EveSong smashed the jug of whiskey down into the fire. The vessel shattered, and what alcohol remained erupted in geysers of flame and steam. The assembled Garou jumped back from the fire, awe or amusement or annoyance coloring their features. Laughter and scattered muttering followed, as they settled back into their places.

"That very same night, while Luna's same countenance graced the heavens, Rainchild and Cloudkill built stone by stone the shrine to Water Snake that we all know. And just as Cloudkill received his name by rights of his battle atop the mountain, this sept receive its by right of that fateful battle that cleansed the land, when the spirits came to our aid and the night was full of the mournful wailings of the Wyrm."

As the fire burned down, the Garou almost as one looked again to Cloudkill—and still he did not take note of them. Grim and unseeing, he stared toward the red-orange coals; like a deaf old man, he did not acknowledge that the story had come to its end. Among them all, he was the one who had started least at EveSong's histrionics with the jug. Among them all, he seemed unmoved by the tale. The others watched him intently. EveSong waited expectantly for the customary howl of approval, yet the silence drew out and deepened—

"Liar!" Black Rindle roared, crashing from his place of seclusion into the light. "Liar!" He let drop his man-face and gave vent to the despair and rage which were never far. "The wailing is not of the Wyrm!" he snarled. "It is of the dispossessed, the tormented!" He kicked at the fiery brands, scattering coals and sparks. "It is for Galia Rainchild, the best of us, who lies dying! All that is worth saving dies with her, but none of you *see!*"

Several of the Garou fell back from the unexpected onslaught. Night Terror stepped forward menacingly. Stands Firm was infuriatingly unmoved, alert, curious even.

Barks-at-Shadows, who had fallen backward, lurched forward now and grabbed Black Rindle's arm. "You mustn't say such things," the moon-calf bleated, panicked. Black Rindle ripped his arm away, striking the Fang across the face.

"There is no comfort here!" Black Rindle shouted. "No reprieve from the Wyrm! There is nothing but—"

Cloudkill's claw slashing across Black Rindle's chest staggered the hunchback. He stumbled away from the fire—but within him the fire burned, flamed dangerously hot. He coiled to spring, but the image of Cloudkill standing tall, painted by the red-flickering firelight, brought Black Rindle up short.

"So many mistakes," Cloudkill said in fierce low rumbles of Garou-tongue. "But one that I cannot escape. All my deeds, my striving, yet I cannot wash away the stain upon my honor. I would give back *all* the stories," he said, claws digging into his own palms, "if it could undo you, if it would cleanse the earth of your accursed being!"

Those who were growling at Black Rindle and the commotion of the scattered fire suddenly fell silent. They held fast, as well, completely still. But to Black Rindle, it seemed as if they receded miles into the darkness. There was none other but himself and Cloudkill standing around the fire. Cloudkill was older and not so large as Black Rindle, but the fury of Gaia and the spirit world burned in the Theurge's green eyes. A thousand insults and curses sprang to Black Rindle's lips, words that he had muttered to himself and hurled at his sire in the relative safety of dreams countless times—but in the face of the renowned elder, courage failed Black Rindle. He bared his teeth, but spoke nothing.

"You are a sign of my weakness, whelp!" Cloudkill confessed to the night. "The way of our elders was right, when they used to bash those like you against the rocks when first you were pulled from between your mother's legs!" For the briefest instant, Cloudkill's shoulders slumped, his energy flagging, as if mention of Black Rindle's dam was too much to bear. But just as quickly, seething hatred stoked the Alpha's fury. "Be gone from this place of honor. You," he spat, "are vile disgrace. You are dead to me, as to the Mother."

Both Garou leaned forward on their wide clawed feet, ready to attack. They breathed rapidly, uncontrolled rage but a word or a harsh glare away. A burning log popped, sending a fiery ember into the air—and by the time the spark drifted to the ground, Black Rindle was gone.

Chapter 7

The deep forest had always been a refuge for Black Rindle. The caern was a place of humiliation, and town was no better. Of the humans, only the children pointed or screamed, but the adults followed him with their stares of pity or groundless animosity. How tempting it was at those times to give in to his rage, to rend their staring eyes from their faces. If the humans only knew how close death lurked, or that they continued to live by the sufferance of Black Rindle...

Tonight, even the forest was small consolation. Black Rindle bounded over log and boulder. He let the fury of the man-wolf carry him, running as often he did until he purged the violent urges from mind and body. But tonight they resisted exile, holding as tightly to him as did the loathing and resentment and rejection that were constantly his lot. The very forest itself seemed to reject him. Clinging vines attempted to trip him; branches slapped at him as he passed, trying to draw the blood and break the bones that were so offensive to Mother Gaia. Brambles tore at the blanket he wore wrapped around his arm. More than once he felt resistance and heard the tearing away of bits of cloth that might just as well have been his flesh. The shadowy trees were stiff whiskers, and he but an engorged bloodtick, or a virulent mosquito, best crushed lest he spread defilement.

Though after so many miles his lungs burned, still he ran. With every step his heart pumped rage through his veins. His fury sprang from a well that would not run dry, could not run dry. All the insults and abuse that had been heaped upon him from the earliest of his days and nights, from Garou and human alike, surged to the surface. The Wyrm take the humans in the town, who were nothing to him! The Wyrm take Cloudkill and the sept! Cloudkill, who had sired him! Black Rindle was not the one who had violated the Litany, yet it was he who shouldered the punishment of the tribes. Let Gaia strike him down, but let her strike down Cloudkill as well. And all of the others. They had spent a lifetime rejecting Black Rindle; tonight was merely the most open, the most public, break. They could reject him no longer if *he* rejected *them*, if he didn't crawl back seeking forgiveness and acceptance.

When finally Black Rindle did pause, he raised his face to the stars which were his birthright—and loosed his anguished howl to the heavens. Let Gaia strike him down if she wished. Here he was. Let his voice be engulfed by the wilderness, as if he had never existed. How much better if that had been the case.

But Black Rindle was not alone. His cry startled other dwellers in the forest. His head whipped to the side at the sound of creatures scattering. He sniffed the air, took in their scent in but an instant: deer, a stag and a doe. And in but another instant, Black Rindle was in motion, his claws digging into the earth, propelling him with powerful, lightning-fast strides. His fury again took hold as he bypassed the trail of the doe and kept to the scent of the stag. His eyes bulged from his snarling, contorted face. Hot spittle ran from his snout, and his breath fired steamy jets into the night.

He closed on the stag quickly but did not pounce at the first opportunity. As much as his heart lusted for blood, those last few seconds when the prey was within sight, *within reach*, were the closest Black Rindle ever came to peace, to equilibrium of spirit and desire. He savored that sensation for a full second, and another—and the stag veered off sharply.

Black Rindle howled again, this time in rage. Even the creatures of the forest mocked him! He clamped shut his jaws and bit through his own tongue. The blood ran thick, his mouth burning. Red haze clouded his vision. His heart, pounding in his ears and chest and sex, nearly burst.

The stag veered again, this time through a shallow gorge. For a moment, Black Rindle lost sight of his prey. He bounded straight up the rise on the closest side of the gorge. Before he regained sight of his prey, he launched himself from the crest. Crashing through spindly branches, he landed full force upon the back of the stag. Black Rindle's claws ripped open the beast's throat before they fully tumbled to the ground in a spray of leaves and dirt.

His fangs finished what his claws had begun and, covered in blood, Black Rindle howled victory to the night.

Once he had carved out and eaten the heart, Black Rindle stood over the carcass of the stag. He raised his bloody claws over his head, then slowly lowered his hands, tracing in the air the shape of Sister Luna in her Ahroun fullness. The ritual, more so than the hunt or the kill or the heartfeast, eased Black Rindle's rage, soothed him. By the time his hands reached his sides, he breathed almost normally, his own heart was no longer about to burst.

"I thank you, stag-in-the-night, for your sacrifice," Black Rindle intoned. "For the gift of your flesh, that my body may be strong in the service of Gaia."

Black Rindle knelt beside the carcass. He gazed into the staring, unseeing eyes of the stag. Despite the darkness, he saw himself on the curved glassy surface. "I thank you, stag-in-the-night, for your sacrifice," he said again. When Black Rindle again stood, the world around him had changed—or rather he had changed worlds.

He stood over the carcass of the stag, but the body was insubstantial, less real here than was Black Rindle; less real even than the ephemeral, translucent trees which shimmered from this world to that as the wind caused them to sway; less real by far than the stars that burned white-hot in the sky, so close that Black Rindle could reach up and touch them.

He looked again at the dead eyes of the stag, no longer unseeing; he followed their gaze, and there stood the spirit of the splendid beast, tall and proud, chin aloft, antlers raised to the heavens. With a flick of his head, the stag brushed aside the stars, which chimed like tinkling glass beads.

"I thank you, stag-in-the-night, for your sacrifice," Black Rindle said a third time, as was proper, "for the gift of your flesh, that my body may be strong in the service of Gaia." He held out his bloody hands, palms raised, so that the spirit could call the deathwind to cleanse them.

But the stag turned away from Black Rindle. The deathwind did not come, and the hunter stood impotently with his fouled claws before him.

"Stag-in-the-night…?" Black Rindle began, but he knew not how to appease the ghost. Had he not spoken the words of ritual? How else might he entreat the aggrieved spirit? Black Rindle's confusion turned hard; it curled in on itself, like a serpent devouring its tail. "Do not mock me, stag-in-the-night," he demanded, having been rejected quite enough already this evening. "I have spoken the words. Now call the wind, so that the blood is washed from my hands." The stag still looked away; it did not respond. *Call it!*

When Black Rindle raised his voice, the stag bolted—but its antlers were tangled: among the shimmering branches; among the stars that clustered about. The stag stumbled, unable to free itself.

The smell of blood dripping from his hands enraged Black Rindle. The stag would flee without having called the deathwind. "Serves you right!" he shouted. "Stupid beast. The trees and stars know that you wrong me. You will call the wind."

He stepped closer, but the stag-spirit reared and lashed out with its hooves. One struck Black Rindle in the forehead. He staggered; he stumbled back a step. His vision went red, clouded by the blood that flowed from the wound.

Black Rindle jumped at the spirit. "You must call the wind. I will free you, and then you must call it!"

The stag thrashed and kicked, recoiling from the odor of its own blood that dripped unabated from Black Rindle's claws, and from the scent of the Garou's blood running down his face. The sharp spirit-hooves slashed Black Rindle on the chest and arms and face. But he did not back away. The more the stag struggled, the more tightly it became entangled in the branches. The stars wound about its antlers, forming a brilliant, luminous sheath around them. Black Rindle's pain and anger mounted until finally he reached up, grabbed the antlers, and snapped them.

The stag-spirit let out a great cry of fear and anguish—but it was free. It turned and fled, its antlers falling to pieces in Black Rindle's hands. "You must call the wind!" he cried after the spirit. He would have followed, would have *made* it call the wind, but now the branches were twined about his arms. Though he struggled and bellowed with rage, he could not free himself. And the stag-spirit was gone.

If before he had run a hundred miles, Black Rindle felt that he ran another hundred now, twisting and pulling and slashing at the branches. But only when he had exhausted himself, exhausted his anger, did the branches and vines slip loose from his arms. He stood slack and panting, blood dripping from his claws as if he had just that instant killed, the glassy eyes of the stag's ephemeral carcass watching him.

"The stag-spirit will not call the wind for you," a voice said.

Black Rindle turned and saw a great, magnificent wolf — magnificently ugly, perhaps the ugliest creature Black Rindle had ever seen, uglier even than himself. The wolf was huge; as Lupus it stood as tall as man-wolf Black Rindle. It peered at him through eyes one brown, one green. It stood awkwardly; all four legs did not seem the same size. And its coat — its coat was the strangest and ugliest of all.

The wolf was many colors, but not in splotches or streaks or mottled patterns. Instead, his coat was like a patchwork quilt with distinct sections in a multitude of hues, as if a thousand Garou had shed their skins, and portions of each were haphazardly reassembled, stitched onto the flesh of this ghastly creature. "The spirit will not call the deathwind," he said again, and cocked his head, perplexed.

"Even the spirits spite me," Black Rindle muttered.

The wolf, cocking his head the other way, looked at Black Rindle. "No," the wolf said. His words seemed to traverse a great distance before he managed to speak them. Perhaps, Black Rindle thought, the wolf's brain and tongue, like the patches of his fur, were from different Garou and were not well acquainted. "It is you who spites the stag-spirit."

The slow-witted wolf's confusion proved contagious; Black Rindle stared at him, uncomprehending and more than a little irritated. "I spoke the words of ritual," he insisted. "It should have called the wind to cleanse the blood from my hands." He held forth his bloody claws as if to prove the point.

The wolf looked at him, and at his hands, but for some time did not respond. Then he said: "I am Meneghwo."

Black Rindle continued to stare. "Good for you." But what did that have to do with anything? He tried to shake the blood from his hands, to wipe it on his legs, the grass, the hide of the deer carcass, but to no avail. Still blood was on his hands, and still the ugly wolf watched him. "I am Black Rindle," he said at last. "The Despised."

The wolf considered that intently, then: "Who despises you, Black Rindle?"

Black Rindle scoffed. "All despise me. Garou, human, spirit. Mother Gaia herself would be better off did I not exist. Doesn't this tell you that?" He twisted about so that his hump, always apparent, was displayed most prominently.

"It does not look so bad to me," the wolf said. He seemed perplexed again by Black Rindle's wry laugh—or perhaps it was merely the different-colored eyes and the tilt of the wolf's head that lent the appearance of confusion. "Were you hungry?" he asked.

"Was I...?" Black Rindle laughed again. The wolf seemed slow, but as it leapt from thought to thought, it was Black Rindle who was left trying to keep up.

"Why did you kill the stag? Were you hungry?"

The question was like the touch of silver. Black Rindle felt as shamed as if he'd been outsmarted by Barks-at-Shadows. The question hung between them like winter-breath. The wolf waited patiently. Black Rindle could lie, but what would be the point? "I was not hungry," he said. "I feasted with my sept earlier this very night."

The wolf sniffed at the air, unconcerned with what Black Rindle had to say. "Follow me," he said, and then trotted away into the forest without waiting for Black Rindle to agree.

Black Rindle followed Meneghwo, the wolf of a thousand coats. The stars continued to dance overhead but seemed disinclined to interfere with the Garou now that the stag-spirit was well gone. Despite his awkward appearance, the patchwork wolf moved swiftly through the forest. More than once Black Rindle lost sight of him, and only by smell did he track the wolf across the Umbral landscape. Black Rindle ran more swiftly, but always he seemed to be losing ground. The periods when he depended upon scent grew more lengthy, his sightings of the wolf less frequent. He was tempted to call out to Meneghwo, but even the lowly creature that Black Rindle was, his pride would not allow him to do it.

Having rejected that idea, Black Rindle nearly ran over the wolf. Meneghwo was sitting patiently, with his teeth and snout worrying a bramble caught in one his mismatched patches of fur.

"You are wrong," Meneghwo said.

"What?" Black Rindle had just kept his balance, and now this random allegation cast at him...

"I do not despise you," Meneghwo said. "So *all* do not despise you."

Black Rindle did not have time to respond before the wolf was again on his way. Black Rindle hurried after to keep up, thinking as he went of Meneghwo's words. If he didn't despise Black Rindle, it was only because the wolf didn't *know* him, or didn't recognize the hump on Black Rindle's back for the curse that it was—or the wolf was simply as stupid as ugly. If he meant comfort by the words, he failed.

When next Meneghwo stopped, Black Rindle recognized their surroundings—but not the way by which the two Garou had come. They stood within the bawn of the Sept of the Wailing Glade, before the stone shrine built by Galia Rainchild so many years ago. The stones were stacked one upon another, forming a wall of sorts. One end dipped into the nearby stream. From there the piled stones snaked to the center of the glade and ended in a short, twisted column—at least, that was how the wall appeared in the mundane world. Here, across the spiritual Gauntlet in the Penumbra, Black Rindle saw the stones as they were meant to be.

From the shallow stream rose a huge writhing serpent, each stone a reptilian scale reflecting the brilliance of Luna. At the center of the glade, the snake held its head aloft, several feet above the ground. Water Snake's mouth was spread open, and perched upon its fangs was an inordinately calm spirit-owl. The bird did not appear concerned about the venomous fangs beneath its talons, nor did the owl seem to coerce the snake into keeping its mouth open. The snake's body wriggled, and the owl, quite tranquilly, observed Black Rindle and Meneghwo. And then the owl spoke:

"Bring her to me," it said. Black Rindle stared hard at the spirit bird, for it had spoken in a voice that was as familiar to him as the moon and stars were to the sky: Galia's voice. "Bring her to me," the spirit creature said again.

Black Rindle did not understand; he was no Theurge born to the ways of the spirit world. He did not know how he and the ugly wolf had reached the caern without passing through places that Black Rindle would recognize, even in the Penumbra; nor had they traveled nearly as far as Black Rindle had run *away* before. He did not know how it was that Owl spoke in the voice of Galia. He thought to question Owl but decided that he had angered enough spirits tonight. Black Rindle did as the spirit bid him.

His steps carried him over ground that was familiar to yet different from what he was accustomed. He'd been born in this glade, interacted with the spirit world all his days, though never had he grown comfortable with it. The strains of silver and violet that wavered beneath the surface of the earth unsteadied him; the stars that danced overhead made him nervous; the giant writhing snake and the spirit bird that sat upon its fangs and commanded him were more than a bit ominous. Yet this place, as much as any other, was a place of the Garou. Perhaps Black Rindle was more at home here than he had realized before—but no, if others of his kind were here, still they would mock him, and this place would become like any other. Had not even the stag-spirit turned its back on him?

Black Rindle had not asked, but he knew of whom the Galia-owl spoke. He went where he had been earlier that day: the hollowed out place beneath the rock. Except here there was not rock. Only the hollow, like a shallow grave. And in it lay Galia Rainchild.

That he could see her, touch her, was dire portent. So far had she slipped from the other world, almost fully into the world of spirit. Black Rindle leaned down to lift her lupine body, and she was as nothing to him. So frail, so light. She could not be the same strong woman who had given birth to him. *This* was her payment: to rot and wither and die. Black Rindle wished that he could take her place, that she could go on living. *He* should be the one to suffer and die. He, accursed of Gaia, was the one who should never have been born.

He buried his face in her fur and wept. Her heart beat still. Faintly. Breath as shallow as her grave. Even so ill, she was a beautiful wolf, though the sheen of her coat had dimmed and her flesh lay slack upon her ribs.

Black Rindle carried her to the shrine. Water Snake and Owl and Meneghwo were as he'd left them.

"So few there are who heed my advice these nights," spoke Owl. "You are one of the last."

Black Rindle was shamed. The tears on his face were as warm as the blood he realized still clung to his claws. He had wronged the spirits tonight, aggrieved the stag, and yet Owl spoke kindly of him.

"Rage and hatred are not one and the same, young one," Owl said. "You must rely on the first without surrendering yourself to the second."

Black Rindle tried to listen to Owl's words, but the spirit's voice took on a distant quality, and vague, as if all of the world were now hollow. And the tenor of his dam's voice after so long an absence drove home the pain of loss and brought anew tears to his face. Then Black Rindle realized that, as he stood before the writhing snake, Galia Rainchild stirred in his arms. She opened her eyes; she tried to form words, to snarl, but could not summon the strength.

As Black Rindle's tears dripped upon her coat, she sniffed at the air; her tongue lolled from her mouth. And then she began to lick Black Rindle, to lick his hands and the blood of stag-in-the-night that stained him still. Where before Black Rindle could not wipe the blood away, now Galia washed him, cleansed him. Not until the blood was completely gone did she stop. She seemed to have gained strength from the stag's blood. She spoke to her pup:

"My Onyx," she said weakly. "My beautiful Onyx."

Black Rindle cradled her to his chest; again, he buried his snout in her warmth. Galia took a deep shuddering breath and spoke no more. For a moment, Black Rindle feared the worst, but he could still hear her heart beating faintly, could still feel her labored breath. Her words, much like Owl's, echoed for Black Rindle. *My Onyx. My beautiful Onyx.* He raised his face to the sky and howled, and the stars danced to the rhythm of Galia's words. *My Onyx. My beautiful Onyx.*

At some point, Black Rindle noticed that the glade was silent. The only sound was that of the words in his mind. He looked up to see Owl and Meneghwo watching him, and another watching him, as well: Balthazar Spirit-Walker stood with hands upon his hips, gaze cold and unflinching. He was tall as Black Rindle, but leaner, his wiry man-wolf muscles suited to speed and endurance rather than raw power.

Why was it, Black Rindle wondered, that this Strider had come among the sept and been allowed to make of Galia his personal charge? He had not left her side, true, but why was he accorded such respect? Black Rindle's hackles rose. "She isn't ready for you, vulture," he said.

Balthazar said nothing, but merely held out his arms that Black Rindle should give Galia over to him. Black Rindle glanced at Owl, and ever so slowly the spirit bird nodded. Black Rindle scowled, but he laid Galia gently in Balthazar's arms.

"I felt you with us," Balthazar said. "And then she spoke...tried to speak. She is so weak, has so little breath."

"I heard," Black Rindle said. He screwed up his face in an effort to dam up the tears. He would not cry before this self-important Garou. But the effort almost undid him.

"I will take her back," Balthazar said.

Again, Black Rindle looked to Owl, and again the spirit nodded. Balthazar turned from them and took Galia away. The Wyrm could have ripped Black Rindle's heart from his chest at that moment, and the metis would not have known.

"So few there are who heed my advice these nights," Owl said again. "You are one of the last." And then he was gone.

Water Snake was a collection of stones, a wall between the stream and a column, when Meneghwo put his hand on Black Rindle's shoulder. "I will take you back," said the patchwork wolf.

Back. Black Rindle allowed himself to be led. His heart was numb with anguish. He knew that it was best he left this place; if Balthazar had sensed his presence, then the others might. Cloudkill might. Yet it was not prudence that moved his feet, but rather lack of will to resist. In what seemed to him no more than a few steps, he and Meneghwo were standing once more above the staring carcass of the stag.

Black Rindle held out his hands, licked free of blood, to the dead stag. "I ask your forgiveness," he said. "I killed when there was no need. No hunger, only hatred."

The stag's body did not move; the spirit did not return or acknowledge the words spoken. But slowly, very slowly at first, then more rapidly, the carcass began to change—to darken and harden. Until it was stone. A forever unmoving stag, throat and heart torn out.

Black Rindle looked upon the graciousness of the spirits and felt keenly that he was not worthy. He cast about and found scattered upon the ground broken shards of antler encased in starglow sheathing. He took the most jagged of these and stabbed them into his chest, offering his blood to the spirits so that it might atone for his misdeeds.

Meneghwo, just a step away, pressed his forehead against Black Rindle's chest, and when the ugly spirit wolf drew away, his face was blood red, as if one piece of his patchwork coat had come from the hunch-back metis before him. "There is not always the need for blood," the wolf said, shaking his head in sadness. "There is no need."

And then Black Rindle stood alone in the forest, the stars far above him in the night sky.

Chapter 8

Kaitlin was wrong about never being hungry again. By the time her finger stopped bleeding, she was starving. She had washed the cut with soap and that had started it bleeding again, which was probably for the best since she didn't have any disinfectant in the house. The bleeding, as long it wasn't too heavy, would get dirt out. Kaitlin didn't have any Band-aids or bandages either, so she wrapped a scrap of paper bag around her finger and fastened it with a rubber band. Twice she added new strips of bag to the old, until the blood stopped coming through.

All the while, she ignored her growling stomach. She was accustomed to being hungry, going a few days without eating. Not until she stood up from the card table in the kitchen and was nearly overcome by vertigo did she decide that she needed to do something about food. Soon. But the sun was already low in the late-afternoon sky, and after what she'd seen last night and today, no way in hell was she hiking all the way to town after dark. The card table was not particularly sturdy, but luckily Kaitlin wasn't tall or heavy; she held on tightly for a few seconds until the world righted itself. In the end, she settled for climbing up the stairs and into bed. This was how she had spent many of her last weeks in the city—huddled under a blanket, safe from, or at least denying, the world beyond—and her first weeks after moving here.

It was funny, she'd always thought—funny *perverse*, not funny *ha ha*—that the monsters that had initially caused her to recoil from the world were all too human. When she'd first begun to see the supernaturals, as she thought of them, she'd been…intrigued. Disturbed but at the same time fascinated. She was seeing things that shouldn't have been there, shouldn't have *existed*: shimmering spectral figures, walking corpses, demons in possession of otherwise innocent people. Yet after the shock subsided, she was always left with curiosity. Sure, some of the beings were more intimidating than others, but Kaitlin wanted to know what they were, where they'd come from, and the harder she looked, the more of them she saw.

Curiosity. She hadn't realized it at the time, but Kaitlin had started with two strikes against her—she was a teenager and she'd lived a safe suburban life to that point, both factors which had made her think she was invincible—and her curiosity had been strike three. More and more, her observation of the supernaturals had led her into the cities: Detroit, sometimes Iron Rapids. The spirits seemed so much more restless there than in the whitebread cul-de-sacs of suburbia. She had known that parts of the inner cities weren't safe, not for anyone, especially a solitary young woman at night. That was the most infuriating part looking back: She had *tried* to take precautions. She hadn't let her mother or brother know what she was doing, of course. But she'd found other people, friends or acquaintances, to accompany her on her strange errands into the city.

Then one night she'd hooked up with some friends of her cousin Clarence. Clarence had grown up less pampered than Kaitlin; in fact, he'd been in prison at the time. His pals had been happy enough to take her for a ride, so happy that they dragged her into the back of their van and gang-raped her.

When she'd made it home again—they'd dumped her in the street and a kind, grandfatherly cabbie had gotten her back, no charge—Kaitlin had crawled into bed and refused to come out. The supernaturals seemed insignificant suddenly, considering what real live people were all too capable of. She gone practically catatonic, and day had blended into night into day…. A few weeks later, when the prying of Kaitlin's mother wanting to know what was wrong had grown unbearable, Kaitlin had run away. And where else had she gone but back to the city.

Looking back now, she could see that she'd been out-of-her-head crazy, but at the time nothing had made sense. For about two years she might as well have been one of the walking dead, because she'd been trying to kill herself. She would have succeeded too, if not for Clarence. He'd found her after her twenty-odd months of drugs and prostitution; he'd beaten her pimp half to death and carried her bodily away.

Back at home, she'd retreated to her bed again. Not too long thereafter, she'd turned twenty-one, the magic number, and the trust fund her father had set up before his death kicked in.

That had been just over two years ago, two years that she'd spent seldom seeing or speaking to another human being. After that, another night of hunger and vague, insidious fear seemed natural enough.

She woke with the first light. The bed where her body had warmed it was so toasty, and everything beyond so cold and ominous, that Kaitlin struggled to get up. But she knew that she had to get food today. She could deny the visions, hold out against them, if she kept herself strong; if her resistance dropped, they would take over, and then the depression and paranoia would claim her again. There was no middle ground between curiosity and despair. Kaitlin either engaged the world or she did not—and the things she'd started to see again urged her down the lonely road of desolation.

Her mind and body were lethargic this morning—too little food, too many monsters lurking beyond the walls of her house. Nevertheless, she pulled on her parka, wrapped her scarf, stuffed her hands deep into her pockets, and abandoned the safety of her home. The wind seemed to delight in picking at her: It whipped under her hood and made the tip of her nose tingle; it tried to hold her back, blowing against her so that she had to lean into it until she thought she might stumble over onto her face. The winter cloudcover was impressively thick and at its most oppressive. Kaitlin wished that she'd moved to Florida. She'd heard it was never cloudy or cold there. No winter. Just bright sunshine all year long, and oranges growing in the backyard, and Disney World. But this was as far as she'd been able to make it from Detroit. She felt old and used up. Probably she'd never make it any farther than this.

She stayed on the far side of the road from Murphy's Tap House, glancing at the building only once. Looked empty, of course. Half the time the owner didn't bother to open it at night. Kaitlin had never seen anyone there in the morning. Even so, she was relieved to be past it. Of the miles into town, she'd only really dreaded the first few hundred yards, getting past that place.

Before long, a misty rain began to fall. Kaitlin wouldn't have guessed that the temperature was above freezing, but it must have been. She would rather have walked in snow than in the fine pelting rain, so cold that it sapped her warmth and strength from the outside while hunger did the same from within.

Well past the bar, she crossed over to walk on the left side of the road. The shoulder quickly grew slick and muddy, so she kept to the pavement except when the occasional pickup truck passed, showering a gritty spray in her face. Sometimes the oncoming truck skirted wide so she didn't have to step off the road into the muck; other times it did not, the driver maybe slowing down and rolling down the window to yell something or spit. The isolation of this stretch of road and the potential danger she put herself in merely by walking to town were facts not lost upon Kaitlin. Not all of the monsters abroad were those that showed up only to her second sight. Not by a long shot. But she had come to realize that to give up on the redemptive capabilities of humanity was never to get out of bed again. If she could ignore and deny the supernatural world, she could not do the same to the rest of creation. Not if she wanted to go on living. She had been down that other road before; she wasn't ready to go back. And so she did her best to keep putting one foot in front of the other, to avoid being run over by passing cars or trucks, and to remember that all the discomforts—the foul weather, the loneliness, the tingling in her nose, toes, and fingers—were all signs that she was alive.

Walking into the town of Winimac from the south, the first noticeable landmark was the steeple of the Lutheran church. It wasn't particularly tall or spectacular, but Winimac itself wasn't spectacular, not showy in the least. The thick stone cross seemed to Kaitlin perfectly suited for the stolid, no-frills town. She didn't feel the same about the lofty, pencil-thin cross on the steeple of the Baptist church on the other side of town—the other side of town being a hundred yards up the street. Kaitlin wasn't sure, but she thought that maybe the Baptist steeple subconsciously reminded her of a syringe and evoked unpleasant memories from her heroin days. So she tried not to be too hard on the Baptists, considering her less-than-impartial perspective was no fault of their own.

Between the bookend churches, the rest of downtown consisted of a handful of well-kempt houses, a hardware store that also served as the post office, the grocery store, and two insurance agencies. Smoke from woodstoves hung low over Winimac, adding to the greyness of the morning and blotting out any other smell. Kaitlin staggered into the grocery store like one of the dead in the city she had fled. A bell on the door greeted her cheerfully. Almost at once she started sweating from the sudden warmth inside. A woman smoking a cigarette sat at a table near the front counter and the cashier, another middle-aged woman and also smoking, leaned against the register. The gaping silence of a conversation interrupted by the arrival of a stranger hung in the air. Kaitlin hardly glanced at them. Her gaze locked on the empty chair beside the woman at the table. Afraid that her legs were about to give out, Kaitlin slipped uninvited onto the seat. The five miles or so from her house were not that long, but she wasn't feeling her best this morning. It seemed that she never was for these trips into town; it took the specter of near-starvation to force her amidst the inhabitants of Winimac.

"Are you all right, honey?" the woman at the table asked.

Kaitlin didn't say anything. She stared at the table, not meeting the eyes of either of the women. The voice sounded as if it had come from the other side of the room, though Kaitlin was only a couple of feet from the seated woman. The heat inside the store and the cigarette smoke threatened to smother Kaitlin. She concentrated on breathing, staring at the table as the edges of her vision grew fuzzy.

"Honey?"

"I'm fine," Kaitlin said at last. "Can you blow that smoke the other way?"

The woman stopped breathing. Kaitlin heard the breath sucked in, a telltale gasp of surprise and disapproval—and then nothing for seconds that might well have drawn out into hours. Kaitlin rubbed her eyes. She wanted her vision to clear. Without looking, she could feel the disapproving stares of the two women. She was tempted to smack the overflowing ashtray off the table. What were these women staring at? Hadn't they ever seen someone who was tired and hungry and didn't want to be suffocated by cigarette smoke? Did they hate her because she was black? They must be Baptists, Kaitlin thought, but then regretted the uncharitable sentiment. Maybe there was a point of common ground.

"My mamma was Baptist," she said with what strength she could summon.

The women's confusion did nothing to reduce their hostility toward her. Kaitlin unzipped her parka and took a deep breath despite the smoke. She just wanted to rest for a second so she could get her groceries and go. Couldn't these women see that and leave her alone?

The cheerful bell saved Kaitlin. The women turned their attention to the opening door, and the smoke retreated. A blast of cold air made it as far as the table.

"Why good morning, Mr. Robesin," the cashier said.

"Good morning, Lois," said the customer, a man almost as cheerful as the bell.

"Running errands for the missus?"

"Just need to pick up a few things," he said. He sounded embarrassed.

Kaitlin used the respite from the women's scrutiny to gather herself. She pushed away from the table. The chair made a horrible screeching sound against the bare cement floor, but she hurried toward the narrow aisles of goods, ignoring the women and the customer. She saw only his shoes.

The store was too small and the aisles too tightly arranged for shopping carts. Kaitlin made her way to the pasta shelf.

"I hope you restocked the macaroni and cheese," she heard the other woman say to Lois.

Kaitlin reached for the blue and yellow boxes, abandoning the few she knocked to the floor. She lost count somewhere around ten boxes, but she was sure Lois wouldn't let her take more than she could pay for. Before her arms were completely full, she thought to check that she'd brought her fifteen dollars. As she reached for her pocket, everything went black.

"Miss?" The voice was very close, but the face, as Kaitlin's eyes fluttered open, was not right. The nose was in the wrong place—No, his whole face was turned the wrong way. "Miss? Are you all right? Can you hear me?"

Kaitlin nodded. She could hear him. The rest she wasn't sure about. This man with glasses and a shiny head was looking down at her, kneeling over her. She was lying on the floor, she realized. "I…"

"You…you fainted…I think. Passed out," he said with a worried, pained expression on his face. "Can you sit up?" He helped her up that far.

"Should I call the paramedics?" Lois asked from the front of the store. "Missaukee County has top notch paramedics. Top notch."

"Ida Hawkin's nephew is on the rescue squad," the other woman said.

"He is," Lois agreed. "Should I call the paramedics? I'm going to call the paramedics."

"I'm okay," Kaitlin muttered.

"Uh…she says she's okay, Lois," the man called to the front. "I don't think you need to—"

"What?" Lois said. "Are you sure I shouldn't call the paramedics? They're top notch."

"Uh…I don't think—"

"I'm okay," Kaitlin grumbled, picturing sirens and lights and firetrucks and ambulances.

"Uh…she's okay, Lois. You don't need to call."

"You sure?"

The man hesitated, looked down at Kaitlin. She nodded. "I'm sure," he said. "She's okay."

"All right," Lois relented. "If you're sure...."

"Ida Hawkin's nephew is on the rescue squad," the other woman said. "Nephew by marriage. On Danny's side."

"They're top notch paramedics," Lois said, relieved that the situation was under control.

"Are you sure you're all right," the man asked, more quietly this time, so as not to re-ignite the debate with Lois.

Kaitlin nodded and started to get up. He helped her. The man, Mr. Robesin, was easily forty years old. His glasses were at least ten years out of style, and his white dress shirt, blue tie, and matching windbreaker screamed industrial middle management. Indeed, there was a small "AgriTech" logo on the jacket breast pocket.

"Are you ill?" he asked, rubbing his forehead, his most prominent feature, his hair having long since retreated to the top of his head.

"No, I'm not ill," Kaitlin said, starting to get a little annoyed. "I mean, thanks and all, but..." At that moment, her stomach made such a horrible, drawn-out, rumbling yowl that it seemed a miracle Lois and her friend weren't interrupted in their recurrent conversation up front. "I just haven't eaten in a while."

For the first time, Mr. Robesin seemed to notice the numerous boxes of macaroni and cheese scattered all about them on the floor. "This is what you eat?" he asked, slightly incredulous.

"Sometimes."

He surveyed the trainwreck of boxes for a few more seconds. "Look, why don't you go sit down, and I'll get together a few things for you?"

"Hey, I don't need—"

"I know. I know you don't," he said, leading her by the arm. "But I'd like to help."

Kaitlin didn't have the strength of will or body to resist as he walked her to the front of the store. Lois and her friend lost their train of thought again. They stared askance, as if the middle-aged white man and the young black woman had stripped and commenced fornicating right there in the center aisle. Mr. Robesin ushered Kaitlin back to the empty seat beside Lois' friend.

"Lois, do you have some hot soup at the hot dog counter?" Mr. Robesin asked. "Get her a bowl, please." He started to walk back among the dry goods but paused. "Are you a vegetarian? You're not a vegetarian...?" he asked Kaitlin.

She shook her head. "No."

"Lois, how about some of your vegetable beef soup? Lois makes the world's best vegetable beef soup." Then he went back and started collecting armloads of groceries, every so often unloading at the front counter and going back for more. "Do you have a can opener?" he asked her. And: "You're not allergic to peanuts, are you?"

Lois was partially ameliorated by Mr. Robesin's compliment of her vegetable beef soup, but after she brought Kaitlin a steaming bowl, neither of the older women spoke another word. They watched Kaitlin, or they watched Mr. Robesin, each woman all the while with a disapproving scowl on her face and a cigarette at her lips.

Finally, Mr. Robesin returned to the counter with one last armful. "What do I owe you, Lois?"

"Did you remember to get *your* things?" she asked.

After his frenzy of confident activity, Mr. Robesin grew suddenly sheepish again. "Oh. That's right." He disappeared to the back of the store and returned with a carton of eggs and a box of tampons. "Just, uh...just ring all this together. And the soup."

By the time he finished loading the groceries into his car, Kaitlin had finished her soup. They walked outside, Mr. Robesin pausing to wave goodbye to Lois who, along with her friend, was watching with stupefied curiosity.

"You didn't have to do any of this," Kaitlin said when they were in the car and underway.

"I know," Mr. Robesin said. "I know I didn't. But I wanted to help. I have two daughters. They're younger than you. But I would want somebody to help them if they ever needed it."

"I didn't *need* it."

Mr. Robesin sat quietly for several seconds. "Uh…where do you live?"

Kaitlin sighed. Need help or not, she wasn't going to turn down that backseat full of food, and she sure as hell couldn't carry it all back herself. "This way."

They didn't talk for the several minutes it took for him to drive her home. Kaitlin figured she must have scared her benefactor. Or maybe he wasn't so friendly after all. Maybe he thought he'd found a poor black girl, and he could just buy her things, and she'd let him hump her whenever he wanted. Kaitlin wasn't having any of that. Almost at once, she felt guilty for thinking such cruel things about him. Mr. Robesin hadn't given her any reason to distrust him—not yet. She wasn't behaving any better than the women at the store. The least she could do was give him the benefit of the doubt. Still, she was wary of showing a stranger where she lived.

When they pulled into Kaitlin's overgrown driveway, she decided that she needed to be civil, at least until Mr. Robesin gave her a reason not to be. "How old are they?" she reluctantly asked. "Your daughters."

"Fourteen and eleven." Thinking of them, he smiled. "They grow up before you know it."

That was as much small talk as Kaitlin was capable of, even with a bowl of soup in her belly. She felt better for attempting conversation, and Mr. Robesin seemed a bit more at ease. They unloaded the groceries, bag after bag after bag. Kaitlin didn't think, aside from in a store, she'd ever seen that much food in one place: boxes and cans and apples and bananas and oranges. When all the bags were stacked in the suddenly cramped kitchen, Mr. Robesin ambled back toward his car. Kaitlin followed him absently; she felt stunned by his unusual act of charity, but a snigger of distrust, remnant of the past, lingered in the back of her mind.

"I can't pay you for this," she said.

"I didn't ask you to."

Kaitlin frowned. She found herself almost wishing that this dorky white man would try to take advantage of her—he would fit more readily into her worldview that way. But he simply smiled and opened his car door.

"If you want a job," he said, "I'm the director at the incinerator over on route 30."

"What do you mean?"

"A job. If you want one. It would start at minimum wage. Office work mainly. Filing. Stuff like that. Can you type?" Kaitlin shook her head. "Well, you could learn."

Kaitlin folded her arms. "Why are you doing this?"

"Like I said, I hope somebody will look out for my daughters someday if they need it. It's the least I can do."

"Least you can do is nothing," Kaitlin said.

Mr. Robesin laughed. "I guess that's true."

"But...thank you," Kaitlin said. That seemed to surprise him. She smiled. "I thought a guy who'd buy tampons for his wife couldn't be too bad." Now Mr. Robesin actually blushed. "You didn't really need the eggs, did you?" Kaitlin asked.

Mr. Robesin shook his head, embarrassed again. "No. I just..."

"Where's your incinerator?" Kaitlin asked, deciding to let him off the hook about the tampons.

Mr. Robesin seemed satisfyingly relieved. "West of town on route 30. If you go in that way," he pointed back the way they'd come from town, past the bar, "and take that first left on Dairy Hill Road, then go left when it hits 30, it's about half a mile. Probably closer than town is from here. Maybe about the same."

"I'll think about it," Kaitlin said. She stood on the porch and watched as Mr. Robesin drove away.

———

Standing in her kitchen, which was now practically overflowing with provisions, Kaitlin felt unsteady. Not the dizziness and weakness in her legs that had assailed her much of the day — the vegetable beef soup had gone a long way toward shoring up her physical strength — but a more profound inner shakiness. It was as if someone had adjusted the vertical hold on her television (if she'd had a television), but not quite perfectly. Every so often, the picture jumped. It happened and returned to normal so quickly, however, that Kaitlin wasn't positive that the scene had flickered. Was everything as it should be, or had she merely grown accustomed to the problem, the imperfection, and accepted that as an immutable part of the status quo?

She tried to ignore the sensation and concentrate on putting away the groceries. After a few minutes, she felt almost giddy, staring at all the food. Her kitchen was a warped scene of Christmas morning. Instead of a tree, she had a refrigerator, and stacked all around were boxes and presents, not toys but food. She filled the freezer with hot dogs and sausage and bacon. The rest of the refrigerator, which had been practically empty aside from the beer she did not drink, quickly filled up as well. The dry goods, cans of ravioli and soup, boxes and bags of rice, pasta, beans, potatoes, she stuffed into the cabinets, most of which were empty, some she'd never bothered to open before.

The sharp knocking at the front door only added to the surreal quality of the day. Kaitlin didn't recognize the sound at first; she couldn't remember the last time someone had knocked at her door. Still clutching a box of Hamburger Helper, she abandoned the groceries and wandered, perplexed, to the door. Mr. Robesin must have forgotten something. Probably a can had rolled under the seat—but why would he turn around and come back after ten minutes to drop off something so insignificant? Unless he *did* want something in return from Kaitlin.

The thought came easily, too easily for Kaitlin's taste—more easily than acceptance that he'd gone out of his way to help her for no tangible reason. She was chiding herself for the suspicion when she opened the door and stood face to chest with a huge wolf standing upright like a man, a body slung over its shoulder. She opened her mouth to scream but didn't have time to make a sound.

Chapter 9

By the time he reached the bottom of the fifth of Jack Daniels, Black Rindle was positive that life had done its worst. Nothing else remained in the way of abuse or calamity that hadn't already been heaped upon him. In truth, he had arrived at that conclusion long before he reached the bottom of the fifth, before he'd taken the first sip. He'd achieved this state of mind previously, many times, deciding that every unfortunate eventuality that could come to pass had. And then, invariably, something worse happened. Apparently his fatalism far outpaced his imagination.

Not this time, though. The brown dregs clinging to the depths of the bottle assured him. Sometimes, when he pressed the smooth glass against the side of his face, he could almost hear the words: *Don't worry about it. Nothing you could have done. The worst is over. Have another drink and forget.*

But the worst was never over. And Black Rindle could never quite leave behind the memories of the wrongs perpetrated against him. Memory was the least of his curses. With enough drink, he could for a few hours block out the contempt others felt for him, but always after the whiskey outlasted its welcome there was still his deformity, the unavoidable physical reminder of what he was: accursed of Gaia, bastard metis of the Garou, pariah, object of loathing and scorn.

"Not this time," he grumbled. "Not this damn time."

He set the bottle aside and pressed his forehead against the bar. Even with his eyes closed, he could see the gaudy flashing of the neon light in the window. The beer sign was the only light Black Rindle had turned on. The Tap House was otherwise in darkness, the pulsing red-orange reflecting from the fragments of glass on the floor. The window had already been cracked; Black Rindle had just helped it along a bit, and once the pane was completely shattered, there seemed little reason not to come inside and have a drink.

"And why not?" he asked himself. He didn't have anywhere else to go; he was exiled from the only home he'd ever known, no matter how inhospitable it had been. Earlier, hours before he'd come to the bar, he had stopped by the girl's house—the girl who had seen him and not run away, the girl who had dropped her blanket. Black Rindle stared at the blanket, which was piled atop the bar. He found some strange comfort in keeping it near him, a relief he couldn't quite explain even to himself. In retrospect, he wished that he'd spoken with the girl, but things hadn't worked out that way.

Sick of a lifetime of what could have been but was not, he raised the fifth and drained it of the final dram. He let the bottle fall to the floor; the container bounced, didn't shatter. Black Rindle grunted, annoyed by his failure even to break a bottle properly. He pressed his ugly homid face against the bar again and ran his fingers through his greasy rat's nest of hair. In a moment, he would fetch another bottle, but for now he stewed in his solitude.

Except he was not alone.

"I expected to find you here," said Balthazar Spirit-Walker, stepping into the mundane world just within the front door of the bar. Shards of glass crackled beneath the claws of his feet. The Nubian stood erect and proud, the leanness of his musculature belying the strength contained within.

Black Rindle stared through bleary eyes. He should be alarmed, he knew—but he couldn't summon the energy to care. "I know this is still sept territory, and I shouldn't be here." The words came with difficulty. His man-form was susceptible to the manipulations of alcohol, which was precisely why he wore that shape so often. "I shouldn't be here," he said again, struggling to lift his chin from the bar.

"That is not my concern," Balthazar said coldly. "Neither Evert's cruel proscriptions nor your petty defiance is my concern."

Black Rindle squinted, trying to clear his vision. Spirit-Walker should have been angry at him, should have threatened to expose him and call the rest of the sept. Instead, the Strider was merely disdainful—and not only of Black Rindle. "Hey," Black Rindle blurted, "you better watch it. That's my old man you're talking about, and he'll kick your—"

"Spare me your wit," Balthazar said. "It is not your father but your mother that concerns me."

The mention of Galia cleared Black Rindle's mind somewhat. He sat upright on the barstool. "What do you mean?"

"I mean," Balthazar said, "that she is dead."

The vertigo of a lifetime of whiskey rushed in on Black Rindle at once. If not for the solid weight of the bar as his hand flailed to the side, he would have toppled onto the floor.

Dead. Galia Rainchild. Dead. His mother, and the only Garou ever to grace him with a tender word.

Black Rindle laughed. His tears were long since spent, and hysteria was as close to emotion as he could. He laughed at his own isolation, which before he had thought was total and now, in truth, was. He laughed at the cruel lightning stroke he had called down upon himself. He had asked how anything worse could happen. Of course such a challenge could not go unanswered. When had Fate ever failed to slap him down when given half an opportunity?

And so he laughed. Balthazar looked on disapprovingly — nothing new there, except the occasion.

"I have informed her mate," Spirit-Walker said, "and I have informed the ill-begotten child of that union. Now I will return her to her people."

The insult carried no weight; it was mild compared to what Black Rindle had heard all his life. But the Strider had said something about Galia, about Black Rindle's mother.... The desperate, drunken laughter caught like gristly flesh in his throat. "You're going to what? What are you talking about?"

Balthazar put his fists to his hips and set his narrow snout defiantly. His jaws snapped, clipping each word, cutting his ties to the Garou he had lived among for many months. "Do you think I came to this place for the enjoyment of your company, or to admire the tyrannical dictates of your hypocrite father?"

"Bold words...considering Cloudkill isn't here," Black Rindle pointed out snidely, but in a way he was envious: He'd never had the courage to denounce his father, except in the bottom of a glass.

"I pay heed to the spirits," Spirit-Walker said, "and it is their bidding that brought me to this dying place. You have heard the story of how your mother came to be here, how she saw the nobility within the breast of Cloudkill and traveled with him. Do you think the Mother of Waters rejoiced when Galia left her people? Of course not. But wise Uktena did not stand in the way. Instead, she sent Water Snake to watch over Galia, and together with Owl he would have made this land and the Garou prosper. But there is no more of wisdom in the Wailing Glade."

Black Rindle struggled to remain on his bar stool. He couldn't absorb all that Balthazar was saying. All the images from EveSong's story were churning in his mind: Cloudkill, the Black Spiral Dancers, Galia, Water Snake...

"No more of wisdom, and now no more of Galia," Balthazar said.

What did Spirit-Walker's words mean beyond the death of Black Rindle's mother? Couldn't the Strider leave the newmade orphan—for Evert had never played the father—with his grief? Why did Balthazar have to go on about the story—the story that never included Black Rindle, that always ignored his existence as an unfortunate, disposable fact?

"No more wisdom," Black Rindle muttered. "I suppose that's my fault too."

Spirit-Walker sneered. He spat on the floor. "Do you think yourself of such great consequence?" He shook his head incredulously. "You are a symptom. Nothing more. Unless you learn to look beyond yourself, then you have already fulfilled your birthright, and Cloudkill was right in everything he said about you."

"Birthright...? I'll show you my birthright, you arrogant bastard." Black Rindle leaned over to reach for the bottle, but he lost his balance and tumbled in a heap to the floor. Finally, his fingers found the neck of the bottle, and he threw it toward the door—but Balthazar was no longer there.

"You are a symptom. Nothing more," said Spirit-Walker's lingering voice, but Black Rindle was not sure if it sounded within the chaos of his mind or in the world beyond him. *Unless you look beyond yourself...*

"But I *have* to look out for myself," Black Rindle sputtered. "No one else is gonna." He started to get up but found that too much trouble, so he sat on the floor and slumped against the bar, his hand resting limply atop the overturned barstool. As if for the first time, he noticed the hand; he lifted it and examined it as if were some disembodied creature rather than a part of himself. It was shaped like that of a human; a casual observer would never know the difference—yet in that way it was not part of him. For Black Rindle did not belong among the humans. He belonged among them even less, perhaps, than he did among the Garou, though how much he belonged among those who had raised him was debatable, as well.

He let the hand fall limp again. During the moments between the bright flashing of the neon sign, he saw nothing. The intermittent red glare made the intervening darkness that much more impenetrable. Black Rindle turned over and over in his mind the news that his mother was dead. In the inconstant light, he tried to find his grief; he tried to summon tears, but they would not come.

———

"And just what the bloody hell do you think you're doing?" Ryan EveSong was not pleased to find Black Rindle sitting on the floor of the Tap House. The Fianna stood in the doorway, much as Balthazar had...how many hours before? Black Rindle wasn't sure of the passage of time; he might have passed out.

"Isn't it enough," EveSong asked angrily, and backlit by the pulsing red sign, "that you can't leave well enough alone at the bonfire, that you can't let anyone enjoy my story—"

"*Your* story?" Black Rindle said, squinting. "Shoulda been *my* story. Shoulda been mine. Never is."

"You stinking sot." EveSong kicked at something in the darkness. The bottle. It clattered across the floor.

"Leave me alone. Can't you leave me with my grief?"

"Grief? I'll give you grief...." EveSong had gained three feet and two hundred pounds by the time he reached Black Rindle. The barkeep's eyes flamed red, even with the beer sign to his back. His string of threats and curses frequently gave way to guttural snarls and growls. "Grief...you bastard...give you...like you've given me...get up...show you grief...." He took Black Rindle by the collar, hoisted him from the floor, and shook him. "…Know…not supposed to be here…away…break my window…rip your…crush your…"

Black Rindle didn't catch most of the invective, but EveSong's meaning and intent were clear enough. Black Rindle knew he should shift forms — that was what EveSong wanted: a real fight. And unless Black Rindle matched Murphy's wrathful Crinos, EveSong was likely to kill him. But for the second time that night, he could not summon the energy. Black Rindle was a spineless rag doll, free of will. He was empty, used up, devoid of any emotion to fuel his rage-beast.

EveSong grew increasingly incensed at Black Rindle's lack of response. The man-wolf's spittle sprayed hot as he barked and yelled, mere inches from Black Rindle's face. EveSong smashed his forehead into Black Rindle's; only a surprising vestige of restraint kept EveSong from smashing Black Rindle's man-form skull like a fragile egg. Black Rindle, stunned by the blow and his mind befuddled by drink, barely noticed as EveSong slung him across the room. He scattered tables and chairs in his wake and lay unmoving on the floor.

EveSong came closer. He towered over the inert exile. His rage partially sated for the moment, EveSong shifted back to man-form. His chest rose and fell with deep breaths as he tried to calm himself. His hands were tightly balled fists at his sides. "Get up, you miserable drunk," he said through clenched teeth.

Black Rindle stirred. "Sure, I could use a drink," he mumbled.

Murphy kicked at him. "Get up! Get out of my bar. You'd best just keep moving. Out of town. Out of Michigan."

"She's dead, Murph. Spirit-Walker has taken her away." Black Rindle thought that perhaps the tears would come now — now that he'd shared the news with someone else. But as with so many other things, he was mistaken.

"What the bloody hell are you talking about?" Murphy snapped.

He didn't know, then. But hadn't Balthazar said he'd told the others—or told Evert, at least? Black Rindle stared up from the jumble of overturned chairs. "Galia. She's dead. My mother. Though no one would know it by listening to your stories."

Murphy kicked him again in the leg, a perfunctory blow, conveying more disgust than injury. "How many bottles have you gone through, you sot? How many bottles of my whiskey? You have one minute to crawl your filthy carcass out of here, and I give you that long only because you're a former septmate."

"She's dead, Murphy. What difference does it make what you do to me?"

Murphy kicked him again. "It makes this difference: I'm tired of washing blood off my floor, so you'd best get your ass in gear. Forty-five seconds."

"Evert hasn't told anyone, has he?" Black Rindle challenged him. "That she's dead. He doesn't care, hasn't cared for a long time. It's all about him and how important he is."

"Thirty seconds."

"And your stories—your damn stories just feed his ego, like he needs that. It's all you're good for, probably the only reason he keeps you around, to make him feel important."

Murphy kicked him again, this time in the stomach. "Twenty seconds. And you better watch your mouth, you bloody—"

"And meanwhile everything is dying," Black Rindle said, still wincing. "What difference does it make what happens to us if everything dies?"

"Talking through the bloody bottle, you ass. And I don't care how many seconds—your time is up." Again, EveSong shifted, back to the uncompromising, rage-driven man-wolf.

Black Rindle saw the fangs, the claws, and from the depths of his emptiness, he welcomed the end.

Chapter 10

One of the last things Kaitlin would have expected of either heaven or hell was water-stained ceilings. She stared at the expansive grey-brown pattern for several minutes before overcoming her surprise at being alive. More surprising, still, was where she found herself: in her own bed, tucked firmly beneath the quilt.

It all came back to her suddenly, and she sat up sharply: the man-wolf at the door, the body slung over its shoulder. She looked around her room quickly, then sat perfectly still and listened for…for she didn't know what. A monster, a werewolf? Whatever she thought she might hear, she didn't. All she heard were the occasional flutter of wings and the tapping of the magpies hunting for breakfast among the leaf-packed gutters of the house.

The sky was light outside, but the sun hadn't made it far enough to shine directly into the bedroom. Morning. Another morning haunted by blurry images of what she had or had not seen. A monster at her door, or simply a smelly, unwashed man? The stench clung in her nostrils like a film of dust, but it was more real that what she had seen—what she thought she'd seen. Like with the owner of the bar, there were the conflicting images of what she saw and what she *saw*. If Kaitlin hadn't left the second sight in the city when she'd fled, she disavowed it nonetheless. But sometimes it snuck up on her; it wouldn't leave her alone. Her months of solitude hadn't weakened it; the visions hadn't withered on the vine from neglect. Could she pretend they didn't exist? Kaitlin pulled the quilt over her head, deciding that she could damn well try.

She stayed that way until her stomach began growling—loud burbling noises, and for once she could do something about it. She got out of bed and reflexively reached for her blanket to wrap around her shoulders—

—Again conflicted images assaulted her sense of memory: the man at the door, not a monster; not a body flung over his shoulder, but a blanket. *Her* blanket. She smelled his stench again and blew her nose on her sleeve, trying to free herself of the unwholesome reminder.

She had passed out. Fainted—whatever—again. Damn it all. And now she'd woken up the next morning, fully clothed, in her bed. She went cautiously down the stairs, stared at the front door suspiciously, as if the temporal and spatial dislocation were somehow its fault. She'd woken up the next morning—in bed, not on the floor in front of an open door. Surely she would have remembered climbing upstairs. Had the unwashed stranger taken her upstairs, put her in bed—? "Tucked me in, for God's sake."

The front door was closed. There were no signs of—of what, robbery? What the hell would he have stolen? Kaitlin ran back upstairs, made sure the cigar box was still under her bed, and that what money and pot she had was still intact. The only other thing in the house—assuming he wouldn't have wanted several months worth of recyclables—was food. She marched back down to the kitchen. Everything seemed to be as she'd left it—except for the box of Hamburger Helper standing upright on the card table.

She had carried that box with her to the door; she'd just not thought to set it down. So he had put her in bed and placed tidily on the table the box of Hamburger Helper she'd dropped. Weird. No, more than weird. Creepy.

Kaitlin knocked over the box. She didn't care for the way it stood there like a monument to some stranger who should never have set foot in her house, much less taken liberties with her unpacked groceries.

Upbraided again by her empty stomach, Kaitlin grabbed a package of corndogs and a gallon of milk from the refrigerator. The oven didn't seem to be working, so she grilled the corndogs on a burner. As she chewed her breakfast and sipped from the gallon jug, an unusual sensation gripped her. At first, she thought it was probably the black stripes of corndog, charred on the heating coil, that were making her stomach ball up like a fist. Then she sniffed at the box of Hamburger Helper; maybe the vagrant's residual stench was making her sick to her stomach.

Not until later, when she was trying to find a place for and put away the rest of the groceries, did she realize that the groceries themselves were the problem—or part of it, at least. Her kitchen was full of food given to her by Mr. Robesin, a man she had never met before yesterday. And another man she had never seen before—that wasn't completely true, but she was refusing to acknowledge that she'd seen him wearing a not-so-human shape that night outside the bar—had been in her house as well. This place that was *hers*, that was her refuge against all that she'd fled in the city, had been invaded, violated, with or without her permission—one of each, in fact.

The realization twisted her stomach. Whether it was the stink of the vagrant, or the unusually heavy breakfast, Kaitlin doubled over. The pain in her belly pulled her to the floor, where she wrapped her arms around her middle. She threw up, chunks of corndog splattering against the linoleum.

She lay on the floor until the cramps eased up. Climbing unsteadily to her feet, she stuck her face in the sink, ran water, rinsed her mouth out. "I've got to get out of here," she moaned.

This place that had been her refuge was now part of her torment.

She was outside before she'd even started to think about where to go. She didn't pause to get her parka despite the chill morning. She stood shivering in the cold and, through the dissipating clouds of her breath, looking back at her house. For the first time since she'd moved from the city, she wanted to be away from her new home. She had hidden herself away, but the world had come looking for her—the *worlds*, both mundane and preternatural.

She turned away from the old house, wondering if ever again it would be able to serve as her fortress, or if the walls that protected her from all things external were permanently breached. With each step, she became more unsure, more desperate. The house was her cocoon; she was emerging, but she was no different from before, no butterfly taking wing. Her insides still were queasy, vestiges of purging, but she set her jaw and continued on, away from the house. This was necessary. She had to face the world—one of them, at least.

"Dear God," she said to the morning as tears began to stream down her face. She wiped her cheeks, but the trembling of her fingers made her angry. Most people didn't have to go through this. *Normal* people didn't have to go through this. But most people hadn't been through what she had; most people hadn't seen what she had seen. That was why they were still normal.

Kaitlin screamed. *"Why can't that be me?"* The harsh, piercing tremors of her voice echoed through the trees. *"Why?"*

She wanted her life back—the life that had been denied her. She didn't care about the rich folks, smug in their fancy houses with their expensive cars and swimming pools and five hundred TV channels. She didn't want that life, their life. She wanted what her own would have been—if she hadn't started to see things, if those men hadn't held her down and robbed her of her innocence and her will. She'd been so consumed by curiosity about creatures from the other world that she'd been blind to the monsters of this world. Damn them all—the living and the dead. And now she couldn't hide from them anymore.

"Keep walking," she told herself. "You keep walking and you'll end up somewhere." She passed the Tap House but didn't look at it. Seeing the cracked glass on the door would be an admission of her window into the other world, and she couldn't handle that right now. Her hands were full in this world just keeping her head screwed on. Her fingertips tingled, remembering the sensation of the glass and the gory image from within the cinderblock building. She noticed the throbbing in her cut finger and wondered if it had just started. She'd not put a Band-aid on it yet; the edges of the slice were pulled apart, the whole area red and puffy. Mr. Robesin had bought her Band-aids. She should have used one, and some disinfectant. But she'd not had a chance: She'd been putting away the damned groceries, and then the knock at the door...

Mr. Robesin. She latched on to his name, his face, in order to keep her thoughts from traveling that other road. He was of the normal world, the adult world that Kaitlin had always assumed she would be a part of some day. As her feet carried her forward, she knew suddenly where she would go. He had offered her a job, a toehold in the normal world.

The thought made her queasy again, but she had nothing left in her stomach to throw up. She kept walking, walked faster along the road. "You've got to do this," she said. Her years of isolation had given her some breathing space, but isolation itself was not the answer; enticing as it was, retreat from the world was not a practical, long-term solution. And maybe the time within her cocoon hadn't been wasted; maybe she *was* different from before. She was stronger, in control of herself— or at least closer to that. She had to believe that she was, or what good was her time away from...from everything, from everyone?

Aside from occasionally wiping her nose on her sleeve, Kaitlin almost managed to forget about the cold. It was not the crisp wind but her intense, desperate concentration that caused her head to hurt. Her eyes were locked on the pavement; with each step she built up a sort of existential momentum, breaking away from the past and moving boldly, if trepidatiously, into the future. When the pounding at her temples exceeded the intensity of her throbbing finger, she began to rub her face, run her fingers through her hair, massage her scalp. Well beyond the Tap House now, she crossed over to the left side of the road so that she'd be facing oncoming traffic. How ironic that would be: to finally venture out into the world only to be run over by a truck.

She stopped suddenly, almost before she consciously noted the fluttering movement in the woods. For a long moment she stood staring at it, absorbed by it; her desperate thoughts were so jostled by the visual non sequitur that her mind suddenly felt blessedly empty. She wiped her nose again. Then she stepped off the pavement, across the narrow shoulder and into the woods.

The underbrush was thickest near the road, where light more easily reached the ground and the creepy crawly vines and brambles thrived. She picked her way carefully through the winter-stripped foliage with just a few snags. The fluttering movement she had seen might have been nothing more than litter caught on a stump and flapping in the wind — might have been, but was not. The object did seem to be caught on a branch but was not a tattered garbage bag or newspaper blown out of the bed of a pickup. It was her blanket.

As Kaitlin moved closer, she saw also what, because of a slight dip in the topography, had been hidden from the road: a body, lying still on the ground.

She stopped. Her brief glimmer of serendipitous joy at discovering the blanket turned to stone in her gut. This couldn't be happening. That couldn't be a body, a real live—or dead— body.

She heard a car pass behind her on the road, and she considered running for help. But she was no more ready for a confluence of ambulances and police and emergency personnel than she had been yesterday in town at the grocery store.

But what if he was dead? She thought about that for a minute. If he was dead, that made it easy. She'd grab her blanket and take off, and no one would be the worse for wear. If he *wasn't* dead—then things might get tricky.

Approaching from upwind, Kaitlin didn't smell him until she was very close. The odor crept into her awareness, like the dead, earthy aroma that would have bubbled up had she sunk knee-deep in black, swampy mud. The scent jarred her memories, brought rushing to the fore visions from yesterday: the man standing at her front door, a blanket draped over his shoulder, *her* blanket. Kaitlin reached out a hand and steadied herself against a sapling.

This was a man lying on the ground, she kept telling herself—not a horrific wolf-thing, not a slavering beast. Looking at him, she knew that he was one of the two...*individuals* she had seen in front of the bar three nights back, but she didn't let her thoughts dwell there. She hadn't lost her blanket at that point; whatever had been slung over his shoulder that night...

He was breathing, she saw. He was bloody and bruised, but alive. What was she going to do for him? She wasn't a doctor. She'd let her own finger, with little more than a paper cut, get gangrene; it would probably fall off any day now, or she'd contract lockjaw and die. Okay, so maybe it wasn't quite that bad, but the point remained: What could she do for him?

Cautiously, she edged around him and to where her blanket was snagged on a gangly tree. She removed the material with care, so as not to tear it; it was already unraveling around the edges. Once it was wrapped around her shoulders again, she moved closer to the body.

She didn't touch it—him—yet; she didn't go that close. His face was swollen, and bloody streaks were still oozing. His left ear was torn mostly off; the ear canal looked to be filled with partially coagulated blood. Kaitlin wished guiltily that he was dead, that she could just turn and walk away. She was somewhat surprised at her own ability to look at the grisly sight. Maybe she was lucky to have thrown up earlier.

Finally overcoming her reluctance, she edged closer still. The unpleasantness of his bloody, battered condition overpowered the unpleasantness of his odor. What Kaitlin had thought was merely the awkwardness of his position she saw now was actually a sizeable hump on his back. She thought at once of a conversation among a group of teenagers in town that she'd overheard many weeks ago. Blackie Hunchback. One of them had called the other that; it had seemed fairly random at the time, the kind of thing that kids call one another, maybe an inside joke, but now it made sense. Kids in a small town, just like those in a city, took delight in tormenting the destitute, the insane, anyone who was severely different. Kaitlin knew....

Blackie Hunchback. He'd definitely seen better days. Kaitlin kneeled beside him. She reached out slowly, touch him on the shoulder—barely. Nothing. She poked him again, a little more forcefully. Still nothing. She sighed. Of course he wouldn't wake up and be okay and wander off on his own—that would be too freaking easy. She grew angry at him, enough to overcome her revulsion and shake him harder.

"Hey, mister," she said, disgusted. "Can you hear me? *Wake up.*" She didn't want to be here; she didn't want to be dealing with this half-dead vagrant. But she couldn't bring herself just to leave him, and after the trouble Mr. Robesin had gone to for her yesterday, she felt bound, if only by karma, to try to help. She leaned close to Blackie Hunchback's good, non-blood-filled ear. "Hey, mister!"

His eyes fluttered open. Kaitlin jumped back. He was able to see the world through only the tiniest of slits; the swelling of his face seemed determined to hold his eyes shut.

Kaitlin spent a moment catching her breath and trying to calm her racing heart, while he, obviously disoriented, looked around moving no part of his body except his eyes.

"Holy bejesus," Kaitlin whispered. She was trembling again, despite the blanket. She wondered if this man who presumably had been out all night had hypothermia; she wondered if he was going to die on her after she'd gone to all this trouble to wake him up.

"Can you move?" she asked him. He didn't respond, didn't seem to have heard, so she asked again, this time speaking more loudly, more slowly, as if talking to a foreigner or an idiot: "Can—you—move?"

His eyes shifted her direction. His tongue moved slowly over his cracked, blood-encrusted lips. He began to move his fingers, but winced in pain. Two fingers on his left hand were bent in places and directions they shouldn't have been.

"Don't move that hand," Kaitlin cautioned him.

His eyes shifted her direction; he seemed for the first time to notice her, to hear her. Maybe it was just all the swelling, but he seemed to glare contemptuously at her; his eyes seemed to say: No shit. Or something to that effect.

Kaitlin grew angry again. "You know, I don't have to do this," she told him. "So you just keep your dirty looks to yourself. You got that, mister? Okay, you don't want to move your left hand any more than you have to. Can you move your arms—just a little. Try real easy. Okay. How about your legs? Are they broken, or can you move them? Take it slow."

Considering how bad the guy looked, Kaitlin was surprised that, as far as she could tell, he didn't seem to have major, life-threatening injuries—which wasn't to say that he wasn't bleeding internally and about to keel over any minute. Eventually, she helped him sit up. Doing so, she realized that her hand was pressed against his hump, and she jerked away. Embarrassed, she took off the blanket and wrapped it around him.

"Don't do me any favors," he coughed, then spit out a thick mix of blood and phlegm.

Kaitlin's anger flared, but she held her tongue. She maybe deserved his ire, but still, she was trying to help; he could be just a little grateful. "You gotta name?" she asked.

He sat slumped forward. Probably he would have lurched back to the ground and died of exposure if she'd left him to that. He was exhausted, beaten, dejected, and looked at her with a tired sense of resignation. "Hunch. They call me Hunch."

Kaitlin could hear the mocking tone of the teenagers she'd overheard; she imagined the taunting refrain of younger children: *Black-ie Hunch-back, Black-ie Hunch-back…* "Hunch?" she said more harshly than she intended. "What kind of name is that? I'm not going to call you that."

He glowered at her. "Blackie, then."

Kaitlin shrugged. "That's a little better, I guess. Blackie. Do you think you can walk?"

He wasn't an incredibly large man, but he had easily six to eight inches and maybe a hundred pounds on Kaitlin. With what seemed to her like an inordinate amount of moaning, they got him to his feet and he draped an arm over her shoulders. Struggling over leaves and fallen branches, she recognized the pungency of old whiskey as one element of Blackie's pronounced scent, one of the most pronounced elements, along with body odor.

"Do you need a doctor?" she asked him. He shook his head. "You're sure?" she pressed. "No point being the big brave man if all it's gonna get you is—"

"Look," he cut her off, "I didn't ask for your help, you know?"

Kaitlin stopped, and he almost toppled over; he would have if she hadn't grabbed his shirt. After a moment they continued on their way, the crunching of dead leaves and the shrill squawking of birds filling the silence.

PART TWO

Chapter 11

Black Rindle wiped the mirror with a threadbare towel, but the glass fogged again almost instantly. He didn't much care; he didn't really want to look at his own face any more than anybody else did.

The world seemed to close in on him—but that was merely the swelling around his eyes making it difficult for him to see. The world, as he saw it at the moment, was a cramped upstairs bathroom in the dilapidated house which evidently belonged to the blanket girl—that was how Black Rindle thought of her: the blanket girl who had seen him and EveSong a few nights ago and not run screaming.

EveSong. Black Rindle stared into the foggy mirror, but the battered face staring back did not move him. He couldn't find it in his heart to be angry at EveSong for what he'd done: beating him and then tossing him into the woods like an old refrigerator to rust and be forgotten. Maybe to freeze, or die. EveSong didn't care. Black Rindle didn't care. It probably would have been best all round if he had in fact died.

Like Galia. She was better off now. Beyond the reach of Evert, and of her deformed offspring. Those who were left behind were poorer for her passing—not something anyone would say when Black Rindle kicked off. No, he should still have been lying in the woods becoming food for the vultures— would have been if it weren't for blanket girl. What was it that had led her to bother him, he wondered, not to leave him in peace? Probably something similar to the reason he hadn't left her lying on the floor last night—whatever reason that was. He'd decided to bring back the stupid blanket. What else was he going to do? Where else was he going to go? But when he knocked and she'd opened the door, she'd freaked out, fainted. Never mind that he'd been in man-form. Weird.

He'd carried her upstairs and left her safe in her bed. But he'd kept the blanket. And then he'd wandered off to drink and get his ass whupped.

Peering into the mirror, Black Rindle wasn't too worried about his mangled face. He laughed out loud. He never had been much of a looker anyway. The bruises would clear up quickly enough. The claw marks would take longer, even for him. He supposed that he'd deserved the beating; after all, he'd broken into the bar. Because he'd been too drunk and apathetic to fight back, EveSong hadn't done him any permanent harm; the Fianna barkeep had just made sure that what he did do *hurt*. Black Rindle poked at the dangling flap of cartilage and flesh that had been his ear.

Behind him, the bathtub was almost full. His broken fingers made undressing difficult, and even with the steam from the hot water, the room was cold. When finally he was undressed and turned to get in the tub, Black Rindle looked over his shoulder and caught sight of his hump in the mirror. He wiped the mirror and looked again.

The hump, more than any other part of his body, more than his swollen face, was bruised and crisscrossed with red slashes. EveSong might have been enraged by the damage to his property and by the refusal of the perpetrator to fight back, but the barkeep also seemed to have been aggrieved by the mere existence of the metis—that was how Black Rindle interpreted the special attention attended to his deformity.

"That's all right," Black Rindle said as he lowered himself gingerly into the too-hot water. "I get pissed about my existence too."

His injuries, mostly having settled into dull aching or throbbing, came alive again, each and every one, with the touch of water. The prospect of soap didn't promise much comfort either. "I knew there was a reason I hated baths," Black Rindle muttered. Maybe afterward he'd find some salt to pour in the wounds, too.

He was taking *forever* in the bathroom. Kaitlin tried to be patient. He was hurt, after all, and moving slowly—and he had *a lot* of washing to do. She wondered when was the last time he'd seen the inside of a bathtub.

She sat on her bed and waited. The afternoon sun made the room comfortable. Every so often, however, she tiptoed to the bathroom door and listened. She wasn't sure what she was expecting or hoping to hear—maybe just signs of life. And that was all she did hear: water sloshing in the tub, nothing dramatic or alarming; just enough to make it clear that someone was in fact taking a bath. Eventually, despite the signs of life, she tapped on the door with a knuckle. "You okay in there?"

"Yeah." No elaboration.

"Okay…. Good…. Okay."

He came out about half an hour later. The first thing Kaitlin noticed about him was what she did not notice: a stench. That much was better. He was still pretty banged up. Soap and water don't do much for bruises and welts. His ear was still a mess; the scratches on his face were clean, but some were alarmingly deep; and he held his left hand braced against his body.

"Your fingers are broken," she said. He gave her a reprise of his *no shit* look. "You need to see a doctor. You need some stitches too."

"I'll be all right."

Kaitlin stared at him, dumbfounded, and obviously a little irritated at his refusal to accept help.

"Look," he said, "you don't give me medical advice, and I won't tell you how to decorate your home."

Kaitlin was doubly dumbfounded. Prompted by his comment, she saw her home as might a stranger: the bare hallway, the upstairs devoid of furniture other than her bed and the bathtub. But who was this ungrateful hunchback moron to criticize? "You can go now," she said.

He paused only briefly, then turned and began down the stairs. He'd put back on the ragged overshirt and workpants that she'd found him in; they were splotchy with mud and blood. After a moment, Kaitlin followed him down the stairs. At the bottom he stopped, but he didn't turn to face her. "I'm sorry," he said.

"What?"

"I'm sorry." He took a deep breath that made his hump rise and fall, as if it were a living creature all to itself. "You helped me. I shouldn't be…"

"An ass?" Kaitlin suggested.

He paused, then, still not facing her, nodded. "Yeah." He started toward the door.

"Blackie Hunchback," Kaitlin said, and he stopped. "That's what the kids in town call you."

"Not just the kids. Pretty creative, huh? How you figure they came up with that?"

"What's your real name?" she asked.

He turned to face her now and stared coldly at her. "Black Rindle."

"That's your name," she said incredulously.

"Yes."

"...You're kidding."

"No."

For a long moment they stood facing one another from a distance of five or six yards. "Well, I'm sure as hell not going to call you 'Hunch,' 'Blackie' sounds like a Labrador Retriever, and just plain 'Black' isn't really much of a name, so I guess you'll be 'Rindle.'" He continued to stare at her. "You're probably hungry," Kaitlin said.

"Yeah," he answered flatly.

She descended the last few stairs and stepped past him. "Come on. You're in luck. I've got a little extra food in the house."

After self-consciously cleaning up the unpleasant mess of her earlier corndog barf, she made him hot dogs. Mr. Robesin hadn't bought any condiments, and he'd not thought to pick up buns, so Kaitlin and Rindle had plain boiled hot dogs on white bread; she ate one, he had the other seven. There was only the one folding chair at the card table, so Kaitlin leaned against the counter. He wasn't much for table manners. He didn't look at her the whole time; he didn't say anything.

Prompted by the uncomfortable silence, Kaitlin's thoughts began to circle and swirl and churn. She started to wonder why the hell she hadn't let him walk on out, less because he'd been snippy with her—which was annoying enough on its own—than because the fact she knew he was...*something*. She didn't understand all of the details. She understood almost *none* of the details. And she didn't want to. She was trying not to think about her visions and what they might mean about him; he was something she'd never seen before. She was trying to ease back into the normal world, though. Not that other one. So she had to think of him as nothing more than some homeless guy who had gotten beat up. But it was stupid to ignore the fact that this guy had *killed* somebody. She didn't have evidence *per se*, nothing she could take to the police if she were so inclined—which she was not—but judging by what she had seen...

"Was that beer in the fridge?" he asked her, breaking the silence at last.

"Huh? Oh, yeah. Help yourself."

"Thanks." He stood up and got two.

"No, thanks," Kaitlin said.

He looked at her, perplexed for a moment, then seemed to realize what she'd meant. At the same instant, she realized that he hadn't gotten the second beer for her. He popped the first can and drank it in less than thirty seconds; the second he finished in a more leisurely minute.

"Thirsty, huh?" she said crossing her arms. "There's more."

"I know."

His clipped, matter-of-fact response set off warning bells in Kaitlin's head. There was something predatory in his tone, something that suggested he would simply take what he wanted. Her fingernails dug into the counter top as quick flashes of fangs and claws and gore shot through her mind. More of her second sight, a residual bombardment? Or a glance at a possible future, events as they would unfold if she allowed this creature to remain in her home? That sort of vision, a prescient glimpse, had not accosted her for quite some time, and she wanted nothing to do with it now. But did she have a choice? Had she cracked open the window to the other world, and now all of those malign influences were free to have at her?

"What?" he asked.

"What?" she sputtered back, surprised, alarmed. "What do you mean, what?" Who was this man? *What* was he? More than he seemed at first glance—first glance to most people. Injured or not, he was deadly. What the hell was he doing here? Kaitlin wanted to claw out her own eyes. How could she have been so stupid as to bring him into her home?

"What's wrong? You looked like...I don't know, like—"

"Who beat you up?" Kaitlin demanded. She was terrified by the flashes of blood and dismemberment that she could not erase from her mind, terrified that he would find her out and realize that she knew his secret, terrified that what she'd seen was not only the past but the future as well.

"What?"

"You heard me," she said belligerently, trying to bully her way through her own fear. "Who beat you up? You didn't just stub your toe out there in the woods."

"You don't know nothing about it, lady," he said, instantly indignant.

Kaitlin sucked in a panicky breath. How far could she push him? She wanted to distract him from noticing anything about her. But how far was too far? If her challenge tapped too deep, into the reservoir of rage and violence that she'd seen, then her vision might well prove prophetic. She couldn't let herself stumble across that line in the dark. Conciliation. "That's why I'm asking," she said, still taut but less challenging. "If you're gonna stay here—"

"Who said I'm staying here?"

"Where else are you gonna go?" Kaitlin heard the words but couldn't believe she was saying them. He was hinting that he was going to leave, and she was convincing him to *stay*? This inhuman killer—literally inhuman—who was likely to gut her and gnaw on her intestines before morning? *Stupid, stupid, stupid.* A minute ago she'd been praying that he would leave, and now she was asking him to be a houseguest!

Rindle apparently didn't have an answer for her question, and she didn't have an answer for why she'd asked it. Again they found themselves overtaken by an uncomfortable prolonged silence.

"Suit yourself," Kaitlin said, finally, and stomped out of the room. She didn't have the nerve to actually rescind the invitation, but she hoped that if she left the door open—

figuratively, at least—his obstinacy would get the best of him, and he'd disappear.

She went back upstairs to her room, pausing only at the bathroom to pick up her blanket. Rindle had left it lying on the wet floor. The cloth was damp and smelled like he had before his bath. Kaitlin changed her mind and left it where it lay. She climbed onto her bed and waited.

And waited.

For a while, she heard noises from downstairs—innocuous sounds, normal moving around sounds; not like Rindle was tearing things up or dismembering people or anything like that. Then the house would grow quiet for a long stretch. She wouldn't hear anything. Straining to listen, as the sun sank low in the sky, she began to hope against hope that he'd slipped out. Somehow, he'd kept the hinges from squeaking, and he was gone. He wasn't going to rape and kill her in the dark of night. He'd had a pack of hot dogs, a couple of beers, and he had gone his merry way.

Against her better judgement, she started to feel sorry for him. She caught herself, and then her emotional see-saw lurched the other way. The questions and the answers kept getting all scrambled in her mind. Why shouldn't she help him? Because he was going to kill her. Why shouldn't he kill her? Because she'd helped him. He would have died out there. He needed a place to stay. He needed protection. But how could *she* protect him? What if whoever beat him all to hell came after him here? That wasn't the point, she told herself. Then what *was* the point? The point was that even though she had helped him, he could still be a crazed killer. No, that wasn't the point either, not the right one. He was different...dangerous...needed help...*she* needed help....

Kaitlin pulled the quilt over her head. She couldn't think straight. She couldn't hold onto a single thought long enough to think it properly. She was a mystified pedestrian with no prospect of crossing a busy highway. This was the chaos she thought she'd left behind in the city. This was what isolation was supposed to have cured. But the world had come looking for her, both worlds....

As she cowered in her bed, she couldn't believe the wrong-headed bravado she'd displayed downstairs earlier. What was she thinking? Was she *trying* to make this guy angry? He was a creature that thrived on rage—

How did she know that? From where had that knowledge come? From where had the images of carnage inside the bar come, when all she'd done was touch the glass of the front door? Kaitlin whimpered. How could she shut out the other world if fragments of it intruded unbidden?

But the other world *was* there. It *would* drag her in. No matter what. She felt the wetness of tears streaming down her face. She might as well have stayed home, stayed near her family and friends. But the world was changing, falling apart, growing sick, dying, and she couldn't stand to see that happen to them. It would have broken her heart.

That was one of the reasons she had left. Maybe *the* reason. She hadn't realized it at the time, and not during the period she'd been strung out on drugs and whoring her life away. But later, during the two years of solitude, she had gradually come to know. Sure, the details of her personal trauma had played a part, but the sense of helplessness stretched beyond the rape. If the human monsters were all that she'd had to watch out for, maybe she could've handled it, but knowing what was out there, what kinds of *things*... What would she have done if some malevolent spirit had crawled within her mother? That's what had happened to Mrs. Mjonksi, two blocks over. Kaitlin had been fascinated by the eerie face that peered out from behind the old woman's eyes—until one day Mrs. Mjonski jabbed two knitting needles through her own eyeballs and into her brain. Or something equally as hideous could have happened to

Kaitlin's brother. How would her curiosity have protected Anthony from the walking dead? She couldn't have taken seeing something horrible happen to her family.

So she'd left them all. And tried to pretend that neither they, her family, nor the supernatural creatures existed. Just like pulling the quilt over her head, leaving everyone she loved didn't mean that awful, horrible things wouldn't happen to them—only that she wouldn't have to experience their pain and suffering. It was selfish of her to leave. But she was too raw; she would have cracked up. *Would* have? Who said that she hadn't?

A creaking floorboard from downstairs interrupted Kaitlin's introspection. She held her breath. After so many hours, weeks, months, alone in this house, she had come to recognize its breathing and settling, the scraping of branches against the roof, the rattle of the windows in strong wind, the rustling of the squirrels nesting in the chimney—as well as the stress of weight on the kitchen linoleum, or on the hardwood of the front hall. The latter was what she heard now.

Her heart was pounding in her ears, a rataplan of twenty, thirty beats, but still she didn't exhale.

He was standing in the front hallway. What was he waiting for? *Get out!* she wanted to scream. Next Kaitlin heard the creak, not of the front door opening, but of the bottom step. Her pulse was drumming her brain. She had to breathe. Curses formed silently on her lips as she tried to breathe—easy, slow and steady—tried and failed.

She followed the progression of footsteps in her mind. The seventh step creaked exactly when it should have. Kaitlin was frozen. She could climb out the window, onto the porch roof, and shimmy down the post to...to freedom? Or to be hunted down in the dark forest? Could she ever hope to flee this creature—

—Not a creature. A man. But she had seen—

A low moan escaped her lips, barely a whisper, but to her ears a scream of primal anguish. A death wail. She couldn't control her fear, couldn't convince her body to move if she tried. She listened again. Had she missed the weight on the twelfth step? It should have been— There. He must have paused. He'd heard her. Probably he wanted her awake when he slit her open and strung her entrails throughout the house; he would be just as happy that she knew he was coming. He would smell her fear-sweat.

Footsteps in the upstairs hallway now. Kaitlin tried to be glad that the hard choices were all made—she'd made them *wrong*, but she wouldn't have to make any more. She imagined what the pain would be like: the claws piercing her flesh, deeper than a heroin syringe, slicing skin and muscle, tearing flesh from bone. She thought that she'd rather be shot—one blast and then nothing—than feel her body rent to pieces. How quickly would she pass out? At the outset, she hoped. But he might save her for later, in that case. Like he had yesterday, not killing her when she was unconscious.

He was standing in the doorway. She wanted to squeeze her eyes shut, pretend she was asleep so that, even if she didn't fool him, she wouldn't see the blow fall. But her eyes were bulging. Was that a tear running down her cheek, or blood from a burst vessel?

He stepped into the room. She felt another horrified moan but held it with her breath. Upstairs was dark. She couldn't tell if he was looking at her. There was only a silhouette. And then he bent down, knelt. He had something in his hands—the blanket. He spread it on the floor, and while Kaitlin looked on in uncomprehending, heart-freezing terror, he curled up beside her bed and went to sleep.

At some point, she started breathing again. Drenched with sweat, she shivered beneath the quilt. Shivered until her muscles cramped—her arms, feet, legs, stomach, jaw. But the cold and the pain meant that she was alive. When exhaustion finally claimed her, she slept like the dead.

Chapter 12

"Is Mr. Robesin around?"

"Yeah. Right in there, kid." The man with the insulated overalls and a clipboard grabbed Kaitlin's arm roughly as she turned away. "Hold on." She started, then tried to pull away, but he had too firm a grip. He held onto her sleeve until a massive dump truck roared past from the direction of the main road. "They don't always watch where they're going real close," he said, as the truck rumbled away.

"Right," Kaitlin said, resentful that he'd grabbed her. Did he think she was stupid enough that she would walk out in front of a truck? But she quickly reconsidered: He was just trying to help, to make sure she didn't get hurt; he didn't mean anything by it. "Thanks," she forced herself to say. She was the one who was a little jumpy this morning. Maybe she *would* have walked out in front of the truck. She seemed hell-bent on getting herself killed lately.

Heading for the small brick building that the incinerator worker had pointed out, she covered her face to keep from choking on the dust that the truck had kicked up. A faint smell of something burning hung in the air; not the distinct flavor of a wood fire, but more akin to the pungent odor of rubber burning, a chemical smell, synthetic. Kaitlin had expected far worse. There was no thick greasy cloud of soot and smoke, no residue of ash settling to the ground for miles in every direction.

She glanced back over her shoulder and saw to her surprise that the worker wasn't still watching her. She felt like everyone was watching her, but a quick survey of the area showed her that the handful of workers among the brick buildings and metal warehouses were busy with tasks other than spying on her.

"You're just freaked out is all," she said, then instantly wished she hadn't. She didn't want these people to think that she talked to herself; she didn't want them to think that she was a freak.

But she *was* freaked out. Rindle had been asleep on the floor when she got up. Curled up on the blanket...like a pet. How weird was that? Not that she was complaining. It was a hell of a lot better than if he'd come upstairs and killed her. In the light of morning, Kaitlin was better able to recognize her overreaction of last night; the visions were easier to dismiss. *This* was the world, the *real* world: trucks and ugly buildings and people at work. This was where she needed to anchor herself. Her mind would stop playing tricks on her soon enough. Maybe if she did well here, she'd go back to her family, or to Detroit.

Thought of the city precipitated a sudden jolt of anxiety. Never mind, she thought. Take things slowly. One step at a time along the dust-choked road.

Inside the brick building was an office packed full of filing cabinets and shelves, and amidst it all, behind a desk, sat a frumpy woman wearing a cardigan sweater. She smiled warmly at Kaitlin. "May I help you?"

"Um, is Mr. Robesin around?"

"He sure is. May I tell him who's here to see him?"

"Kaitlin Stinnet, but...but I don't think he knows my name. He offered me a job."

"Oh. Filing? That's wonderful. I've been after him for months to get us some help. I'm Frances. Just one second." She dialed an extension on her phone. "Floyd, there's a young woman here about the filing job. Kaitlin Stinnet." Frances hung up the receiver. "He'll be right out."

Kaitlin nodded. She busied herself looking around the room and trying not to notice that, unlike the men outside, Frances *was* watching her—not like the women at the store had, full of suspicion and tabloid curiosity; Frances was all smiles.

"Excuse the mess," the secretary said, seeing Kaitlin's seeming interest in the various file drawers and shelves bulging with official-looking papers. "You see, what we do here is create paperwork. The incinerator is supposed to keep stuff out of the landfills, but we have our own landfill right here." Frances laughed good-naturedly and patted one of the stacks of files on her desk. "I couldn't begin to tell you how many trees must have passed through this very office in the past year, but I bet we could reforest from here to Texas and still have a filing cabinet left over."

Kaitlin nodded again. She felt like she was supposed to say something, but she didn't know what. Somewhere over the course of her self-imposed solitude, she'd lost any knack for small talk; she'd lost her knack for *people*. She was so used to being by herself, not having to talk to anybody. What did this Frances want from her? Why was the woman being so friendly? She must *want* something. People were cruel by nature, friendly when it suited them.

"You live nearby?" Frances asked.

There it was: someone else wanting to know where Kaitlin lived. What for? "Not too far," she said, starting to have second thoughts about this whole venturing-back-into-the-world thing. Maybe this wasn't such a good idea, she thought, as she watched Frances' smile grow stiff and slightly strained.

"Lived here long?" Frances asked.

"A while."

"Oh. I see. That's nice."

"Ah, Kaitlin," Mr. Robesin said, opening the door opposite the one she'd come in and stepping into the room. "I'm glad you came. I didn't think to ask your name the other day, but I thought it had to be you. You've met Frances, then."

"Yes," Kaitlin said, suddenly embarrassed by her paranoia. Maybe it was just first meetings that were so hard and she'd already gotten over most of her distrust of Mr. Robesin, but he seemed so friendly and genuinely pleased to see her. "She's been very, um…helpful. And friendly."

"Of course she has," Mr. Robesin said. "So, can you stay and work today, or did you just want to get a feel for the place?"

"Um…I can stay, I guess."

"Great. We'll worry about your paperwork later: you know, W-4, I-9, all that." Mr. Robesin rubbed his hands together. "Frances, can you get her started, help her learn the different reports, where they go?"

"I'd be happy to."

"Great. Like I said, Kaitlin, we'll have to start you at minimum wage, but you'll have a review and possibly a raise every quarter. Fifteen hours a week. We're pretty flexible as far as schedules. We just need help digging out from under this avalanche of paperwork," he indicated the entire room, "and staying dug out. Filing may not seem important, but we're constantly treading water."

"Floyd," Frances said, "you're mixing your metaphors."

"Hm? Oh. Well, you get my drift. Anyway, we're glad to have you. I'll leave you in Frances' capable hands. I have some things to take care of. When I finish up, I'll give you a tour. Sound good?"

Kaitlin nodded. She was fairly stunned by Mr. Robesin's almost manic and good-natured flurry of activity, like in the grocery store, except then she *had* been stunned, and faint.

"Great," he said, straightening his tie. "Then I'll leave you two to it."

"All right, dear," Frances said when the two women were alone. "We'll just take everything nice and easy. There's no need to rush, because you'll never catch up, not in a month of Sundays. But every little bit helps. So we'll start with this pile…"

Black Rindle woke without the familiar hurt of a hangover— which was not the same thing as being free of pain. Not by a long shot . His ear, what was left of it, had bled on the blanket while he slept; his face, though the bruises and swelling were miraculously gone, was a crisscross of weeping, crusty scabs. His two fingers that had been broken were back to normal, if a little stiff. The gashes, even the ragged ear, would heal soon enough, probably by tomorrow, the next day at the latest.

EveSong, angry as he'd been, had made sure not to do lasting damage. Black Rindle would likely have a few scars to remember the beating—his ear, a few light traces on his face, not to mention the criss-crossed rakes on his hump, which at least wouldn't show—but he was lucky to be alive at all. Too drunk and despondent to fight back, EveSong could have killed him. Easily. But the Galliard had restrained himself.

"Dumb luck, that," Black Rindle said. "Everybody would've been happier."

The sound of his caustic words made clear how achingly empty the house was. He had heard the girl get up and leave earlier that morning, but this was a hollowness that transcended her physical presence or absence. Even when she was there, in the room, Black Rindle felt as if he might very well be alone. It was strange: He felt as if he could see right through her, as if she didn't cast a shadow of her own. He didn't even know her name.

He growled to himself. What difference did it make what her name was? She was just a human.

No, he thought. She wasn't *just* a human. She had seen him in the shape that humans simply could not comprehend. Reason fled them. Their minds snapped. Yet that night he and EveSong had come out of the bar, she had not run; she hadn't fallen to the ground like a gibbering idiot. She wasn't *just* human.

She was light, insubstantial, there but not there. Could she be of the spirit world? He was no crescent moon, but the spirits had been agitated lately. Owl and Water Snake had both made themselves visible to him, and Meneghwo—Black Rindle suspected that ugly wolf was closer to spirit than Garou. He pondered the possibility for a great while: that the girl was some type of spirit…. Doubtful, he kept thinking. Why would she want to masquerade as human, a race so often at odds with Gaia's best interest? But there was definitely *something* atypical about her. He couldn't ferret it out by smell, and having met her and spoken face-to-face hadn't enlightened him. Still…

Looking around, Black Rindle could see the signs of her ethereal nature—or rather the signs he *didn't* see proved the point. To his eyes, the girl left practically no sign of her passing, no footprints. She left literal footprints—the kitchen floor was filthy with them—but the house where she lived might as well have been abandoned, for all the impression she left. Slowly, methodically, Black Rindle made his way from room to room. The bathroom and bedroom were the only rooms that she used upstairs, and the only evidence there of habitation: a few toiletries on the counter; one threadbare towel; a cardboard box with an extra shirt and underwear; a slept-in bed; and beneath that, a cigar box with a little money and a ziplock bag of pot.

He left the box where he found it, the contents undisturbed. The money wouldn't have gone very far, and he wasn't interested in the marijuana. More than that, though, the box seemed to him a tiny shrine or reliquary hidden away, inscribed not with runes of the Garou, instead proclaiming: *King Edward Imperial.* The girl, unlike most humans, possessed so little, and these few items were what held power for her, her fetishes.

Downstairs was much the same story. Only the kitchen and the adjacent room packed full of cast-off containers showed any signs of habitation. The rest of the house was dusty, cold, and dark. In the kitchen, the cabinets stuffed with dry goods seemed out of character, and sure enough there was another human scent on most of the boxes and cans. Black Rindle had caught a trace of the scent last night, but had not paid close attention, a bad habit that he knew he should remedy.

The food, unlike the personal items under the bed, did not strike Black Rindle as off limits. Human victuals might not be as fulfilling as a hunt, but they had the advantage of being stationary and at hand. He promptly forgot about the girl altogether, and concentrated instead on the bounty of her kitchen.

"Watch your step!" Floyd Robesin pointed at yelled over the noise of the truck rumbling past. "They don't always watch where they're going!"

At least he didn't grab her arm. Kaitlin had to laugh: all of these men suddenly trying to take care of her, and all afraid that she couldn't look out for traffic. Even so, she was relieved to be outside after a couple interminable hours of filing. She watched the truck roar down the road. "That wasn't a dump truck. That was like an oil truck or something."

"Chemicals," Floyd said. He led her along the gravel road, away from the office and the state road, deeper into the complex. "This will be a quick tour," he said. "We'll just do the highlights. You've already seen the office—probably more of it than you would have liked. That leaves the pit and the incinerator itself, the lab, and the reclamation facility."

"What do you need a lab for?" Katilin asked. "Aren't you just burning garbage?"

"Yes and no. This is what you would call an 'eco-friendly' incinerator complex, state of the art, ahead of the curve scientifically, really. We're testing some experimental technologies and treatments that will be widespread across the country within ten years. You'll be able to say you were here on the ground floor when it started," he said with a facetious wink.

"Uh-huh."

"We're a hazardous waste repository for twelve counties," Floyd continued, unconcerned about Katlin's failure to match his enthusiasm.

"You mean, like...radioactive?"

"Hm? Oh, no, no, no. Not *that* hazardous. We're not a toxic waste site. Our combustion and filtering prevents harmful metals and chemicals from contaminating the air and the groundwater. Mercury, PCBs. We handle a lot of household and industrial garbage—batteries, fluorescent units, medical waste, fertilizers, old paint caches, dismantled electric transformers.... That kind of thing."

"Uh-huh. And the stuff doesn't get into the atmosphere when you burn it?"

"Nope. That's the whole point. Come on."

The gravel road continued a short distance. Past one of the corrugated metal warehouses, Kaitlin and Floyd caught up with the chemical truck that had passed them. Behind a chain link fence topped with barbed wire, workers dressed in what looked like space suits from the late late movie were attaching thick hoses from the truck to valves on the side of a brick building much larger than the office.

"That's the lab," Floyd said. "Access restricted for safety reasons. They're unloading the compounds that are used to form our chemical sorbent. It's injected with a water and limestone mixture in the scrubber—that's the step after the furnace—and damps down the flue gasses and acid gasses. This…" he said, leading her toward a low cement building with a tall smokestack several hundred yards away, "is the incinerator itself. Would you like to see how it works?"

"Sure," Kaitlin said. "Beats filing." She cringed as soon as the words left her mouth. Floyd—she couldn't think of him as Mr. Robesin now that she'd heard Frances calling him Floyd—had given her a job; the least she could do was not bitch about it in front of him.

But Floyd laughed and took the comment in stride. He seemed to enjoy getting out of the office and giving the tour as much as Kaitlin enjoyed being done with filing for the day. It was tedious, brain-deadening work, but what else was she going to do? How else was she going to reinsert herself into the normal, everyday world? And Floyd was nothing if not normal. His glasses made him look a little like a frog, an image his balding head did nothing to dispel. He was a pleasant enough frog, but a frog nonetheless. Kaitlin was still slightly suspicious of how completely friendly he was, how totally *nice*. The same went for Frances. People just didn't act that way—not to Kaitlin.

Floyd took her to the edge of "the pit," where a truck was unloading its cargo of garbage. He pointed out the crane that would move the garbage to the tilt floor, which would slide the load into the furnace itself. Standing beside the pit, Floyd seemed not to notice the smell that made Kaitlin constantly wrinkle her nose.

"You'd think it would be warmer this close to the furnace, wouldn't you?" he asked. "The temperatures are so extreme, the insulation technology is remarkable. It has to be. Otherwise, the building, the cement, would start to break down. Trees a hundred yards away would burst into flame."

"Wow."

"Wow is right." Floyd pointed out the scrubber mechanism, the large tank where the chemical dampener was introduced, and he tried to explain more of the filtration process, but by this point Kaitlin's head was starting to hurt—maybe from the cold, or from the filing, or from all the techno-garbage terms he was tossing at her—and she didn't catch many of the details.

"This is perhaps the best part," Floyd said, leading her beyond the incinerator to an area full of stacks and stacks of cinderblocks. "What does this look like to you?"

"I don't know. Construction zone? They gonna build another building?"

"What they're constructing are the cinderblocks. What do you get when you burn something? What's leftover?"

"Nothing. Well...ash."

"Right. Ash. *Cinders.* In the past, by filtering hazardous substances out of the gaseous byproduct—smoke—incinerators were left with very dense, extremely toxic amounts of ash. The beauty of the AgriTech system is that we separate out the toxins completely. So the air emissions are environmentally safe, and the ash byproduct is non-toxic as well. Basically, we're turning garbage into building materials. And next year we're going to add boilers and a steam turbine generator, become a WTE—waste-to-energy facility—and plug into the local power grid."

"Sounds...impressive," Kaitlin said, knowing that she was supposed to be impressed. "But you still have some toxic stuff, right? I mean, it's not in the smoke and it's not in the ash, but it's somewhere."

"Oh, yes. But the volume is exponentially reduced compared to if we had to dispose of tons and tons of tainted ash. *And* the boys in the lab are working on synthetic applications that break down the toxin altogether and render them inert. I'm not familiar with all the science involved—"

"Yeah, me neither. Hey, are you getting cold?" Kaitlin asked.

"What? Oh, I'm sorry. I've kept you out here a long time, and here I was saying this was going to be a short tour. Let's get you back inside, and we'll work out your schedule with Frances."

Chapter 13

Kaitlin smelled the beer as soon as she opened her front door. The odor brought back half-buried memories. There was a twinge of fondness, too—and that was why she wished the memories were fully buried. She found Rindle in the kitchen sitting at the card table. He was bleary-eyed and surrounded by a considerable collection of empty and overturned beer cans. She stood in the doorway and glared at him. He regarded her disinterestedly.

"What the hell…?" She had seen worse. She had *been* worse, but not in this house. "What is all of this?" she asked.

"You're back," Rindle said. "If you were ever really here."

"*What?*" She did a quick mental count of the cans. "That was a case of beer."

Rindle spoke slowly, deliberately, but still his words were slurred. "No. Twenty-one. Two last night makes twenty-three. You were one shy of a case before I showed up."

"Yeah, and now I'm a case shy of a case. What are you doing?" She kicked at a couple of the empty cans that had found their way onto the floor. He looked at her quizzically, not understanding the question. "Do you know why that beer was there?" she asked.

He stared with deepening perplexity.

"That beer," she explained, not at all pleased, "that case of beer that I bought, has been in that refrigerator since I moved into this house two years ago. I drank one my first night here, and that was the last beer I'll ever have, the last alcohol I'll ever have."

Rindle stared at her and blinked. His brow furrowed. "I don't underst—"

"Obviously not," she snapped. "I stared those cans down every day for two years, and whatever else I don't know, I do know that they don't have any hold over me. Not any more."

"Why…why have it and not drink it?"

"If you don't understand, then my telling you isn't going to make you understand. Not drinking is my way of…*was* my way of, I don't know …of being in charge. I could look at those cans and know that I was better than that. I could take them or I could leave them. My choice."

Light began to dawn in Rindle's eyes. He nodded slowly. "It was a shrine."

"*What?*"

"It was a shrine to strength of will," he continued, no longer aloof but morose, "and I desecrated it. You'll want me to leave now."

"What are you…? You are really weird. You know that?" Weird, she thought, and lethal. Images of him standing before the bar, a body over his shoulder, began to process through her mind. The late-afternoon winter sun was practically gone, and her daytime rationalizations quickly began to give way before the fears of night. Why was she challenging this killer? Just because he hadn't killed her last night didn't mean he wouldn't tonight. Yet there was something infuriating in both his sarcasm of last night and his remorse tonight. "You're pathetic, too," she said before considering the wisdom of her words. "Weird and pathetic."

He started to get up from the card table, leaning on it heavily enough that it bowed dangerously. "I was wrong," he said, dismayed. "That wasn't your shrine upstairs. *This* was your shrine, and I destroyed it."

"*What* are you talking about?" Kaitlin tossed up her hands. "Look..." She stepped forward, put a hand on his shoulder and pushed him. Despite Rindle's enormous size advantage, he wasn't at his most stable, and he toppled back onto the chair. "You can leave if you want to," Kaitlin said with a sigh, "but you're welcome to stay. You didn't destroy anything. You just drank some beer that I wasn't going to drink. Ever." Even as she spoke the words, the voice in the back of her head—the voice of reason, the voice she routinely ignored—was shouting at her to *let—him—go*. Maybe it was the fact that he was so pathetic; she didn't often come across people more pathetic than herself. For whatever reason, she wanted him to stay. "I know you're...different," she said.

Rindle raised his face and regarded her with narrowed eyes. Kaitlin suddenly felt that she'd said exactly the wrong thing. Her sympathy of a moment before was washed away by a fresh wave of fear. The breath caught in her throat. Why had she let the fact that he slept on the floor on a blanket lead her to believe that he was safe?

"What do you mean?" he said. He didn't seem so drunk any more, so helpless and harmless.

Now that she was the one being challenged instead of doing the challenging, Kaitlin felt all the air go out of her lungs. "I didn't mean anything."

"Do you mean different because of this?" He twisted so that his hunch was clearly visible.

"No, I...I didn't mean anything."

"You did mean something. What?" His voice was low, menacing.

Kaitlin took a step back from him. She saw sudden flashes of the inside of the bar: a man's intestines strung along the floor, a hairy black beast gnawing those intestines. She said nothing. What *could* she say? If she told the truth, if she revealed her secret, would he disembowel her? Would he leave parts of her body spread throughout the house for the rats? She backed slowly out of the room, fearing that he would spring on her any second.

Black Rindle watched her back away. He found himself watching her as he would prey. Her timidity pricked his hunting instincts. Would a spirit creature fear him? Spirits were difficult to predict. Maybe she was a weak, broken spirit. Still, one offended denizens from beyond the Veil, even seemingly weak spirits, at one's own risk.

Once she was out of his line of sight, Black Rindle heard her hesitant steps turn to full-fledged flight, as she ran up the stairs. The floorboards of the hallway above his head barely creaked, she was so light, so insubstantial. He knew what she would do even before he heard the squeak of a bedspring. She was huddled beneath her quilt. It was her place of refuge. That was why he'd made the mistake about the beer. The items in the cigar box were but tokens of the mundane world, and while stealing them would have angered her, he had violated what was of spiritual import to her, the beer in the refrigerator — important to her for reasons very different from the reasons alcohol was important to him. Or perhaps not so different.

Black Rindle realized several minutes later that he was still staring at the doorway, the last spot that he'd seen her. He was confused by her alternating bouts of concern for and antagonism toward him. She'd grown angry at him, but then refused to throw him out. He remembered seeing her that night on the road. She had been afraid, but she hadn't fled; she'd frozen, but not succumbed to the complete breakdown afflicts humans upon seeing a Garou revealed. And now, somehow, she knew. She'd said that he was different; she hadn't been talking about his deformity. Maybe she'd known from the start. But how? She saw what humans could not see. Again, how?

He willed himself up from the flimsy table. The alcohol was still winding its way through his body and brain. A quick shift to Crinos would take care of that, would burn the toxins from his body, but Black Rindle preferred the more surreal vision of the world; it masked a few of the harsher edges. Clarity was not a friend.

Once he was moving, he noticed a faint scent that had not caught his attention before—an insidious, unwelcome scent. He sniffed at the doorway where the girl had stood. Now that he was aware of the smell, it was as obvious as the hump on his back. He followed the lingering odor up the stairs and to the darkened bedroom. With each step, he grew more curious about the woman—and, for the first time, actively distrustful of her.

"You haven't eaten," he said from the hallway, trying to provoke some response. He needed to see her, to talk to her—in light of this new scent that pricked up his hackles. "You can't go to bed yet. It's too early." The girl didn't respond, but he could tell that she was not asleep. "What's your name?" he asked. "You never told me." He knew she'd been holding out on him, but how much?

"Kaitlin." She was still hesitant, but talking at least. "You never asked," she said weakly, not very convincingly defiant.

"Kaitlin, where did you go today? You stink."

There was a long pause. Among the deepening shadows, she sat up in bed, letting the quilt fall away. She was still fully dressed. *What* did you say?" she asked.

"I said—" he began in a more accusing tone—before she cut him off.

"You didn't smell so good yourself when I found you," Kaitlin snapped. She lay back down, roughly, almost throwing herself against the mattress and yanking the quilt back up over her shoulders.

Black Rindle was caught off guard by her renewed combativeness. Just a few moments ago, she'd seemed in fear of him. Now...? He found himself growing angry with her; his fingers digging into the wood of the doorframe, he struggled to fight down that most familiar of emotions. After all, what if she *was* some type of spirit creature? Did he really want to piss her off? He tried again: "I didn't mean... *You* don't stink. You smell like something that's...bad. No, I mean...something that's...something you shouldn't...something that's not you." How did she manage to make everything so difficult? Wyrm-tainted, he wanted to say, but if she was truly innocent that would mean nothing to her. He told himself to remember that she likely wasn't as innocent and helpless as she pretended, not if she had somehow overcome the Delirium. "Where did you go?" he asked again.

"I went to work," she said.

"You will not go back." It was that simple. He was willing to give her the benefit of the doubt and believe that she wasn't a clever minion of the Wyrm, that the smell of Wyrm-taint clinging to her was incidental somehow.

Apparently the matter was not so cut and dried in Kailtin's mind. "Look, you," she said with quivering voice, wavering between fear and resentment. "You're welcome to stay here, because I don't think you have anywhere else to go, and I don't like the idea of you getting beat up again and freezing to death. But you are *not* welcome to tell me what to do. Got it? If you're gonna kill me, go ahead and get it over with, but I've had enough of the you-Tarzan me-Jane routine."

"What did you say?"

The last of Kaitlin's defiance drained from her body. She raised a hand, trembling, partway to her mouth, as if she could have held back the words already spoken.

"What did you say?" he challenged her again. She gawked, speechless and slack-jawed. "Did you say if I was going to kill you?"

Kaitlin regarded him with wild-eyed frenzy for an instant, the attitude of an animal trapped, but then when he made no move against her, she grew calmer slightly. Still suspicious, wary, fearful. She drew in a deep breath and spoke falteringly. "Isn't that what you do?"

The question, the *accusation*, hung between them, pushing them apart with the invisible force of similarly charged magnets. Black Rindle was torn: He wanted to press the issue, find out exactly what she knew. But also, despite the stench of corruption that lingered about her, he couldn't really make himself believe that the girl was of the Wyrm. Looking in her eyes, this wasn't how he wanted her to look at him. He didn't want to intimidate her; he didn't want her to be afraid of him.

"I've never killed anyone who didn't deserve it," he said, knowing at once that the words didn't come across how he meant. How was *that* supposed to comfort her? Silently he cursed himself.

With a sigh, Kaitlin let her shoulders slump forward, her tiny frame exhausted by the alternating tumult of anger and terror. All that seemed left to her was resignation. She stared at the floor. "This place," she said, "is all I have left." She paused, took a deep breath. "It was kind of like…like a fortress. I was stupid enough to bring you in, so…if here isn't safe anymore…" She took another slow, deep breath. "Well, like I said, if you're going to kill me, go ahead and get it over with."

Black Rindle cringed at the stark despair of her words. He recognized all too well the mix of fear and resentment that sapped her will. He recognized himself just a couple of nights ago, waiting for EveSong to kill him, *hoping* that EveSong would kill him. Black Rindle stepped toward her. He lifted a hand and, very hesitantly, placed it on her shoulder. "I will not harm you,

Kaitlin," he said in somber tones. "You took me in when no other would. I abused your hospitality and...I am sorry. I am sorry for ordering you about—but a scent clings to you tonight of..."

"Of garbage." she muttered, still despondent, defeated. If a hint of relief existed beneath her despair, Black Rindle couldn't detect it. "I was at the incinerator today, my job," she said. "They burn stuff. That's what incinerators are for. I had planned on taking a bath, thank you very much."

Her attempt at sarcasm encouraged Black Rindle, showed him that she hadn't yet completely withdrawn into helplessness—as he often had. "It is not that type of smell," he said shaking his head. "Perhaps you wouldn't notice. Perhaps it isn't the type of thing you would know."

Kaitlin shrugged. "Have you really ever killed somebody?" she asked, sounding as if she wanted him to tell her that he was joking.

"Why do you ask?" Black Rindle watched her closely. Was she really so unconcerned about the Wyrm-taint? Was she trying to distract him, or did she simply not understand that of which he spoke? He wanted her to tell him that she'd seen him wearing the shape of the man-wolf. He wanted her to admit that she knew. Then, perhaps, he could trust her.

She hesitated, but wouldn't give in. "Seems like a reasonable thing to want to know about somebody staying in your house."

Black Rindle folded his arms, displeased at her continuing dissimulation. She was holding out on him still, this woman who had seen through the Delirium. Yet he couldn't convince himself that she was an enemy, a threat. Was this reason, or unwarranted sympathy for a person who had taken him in? Black Rindle turned from her and went back downstairs. He had said as much as he dared for the time being.

He waited downstairs while he heard, above, the sounds of her bath. She came down later, and they ate in silence. Three hours after she went back upstairs, he followed. He saw her sleeping—she *was* sleeping this time—and he curled up with the blanket on the floor next to her bed.

Chapter 14

There would be no songs of this morning's exploits. Of that, EveSong was certain. Little enough glory was to be won in the slaughter of helpless, stupid beasts.

Still, a hunting raid against domesticated, spiritless bovines was preferable to remaining at the caern. Now that Galia was dead and gone—and Balthazar gone with her—Evert Cloudkill had sunk deeper into his introspective malaise. If the hunting pack was abroad, that only left Barks-at-Shadows, and EveSong could only take a certain amount of the moon-calf. Not that the hunting pack was an ever-flowing stream of intellectual discourse.

"No humans, no Wyrm," Shreds Birch had said in way of inviting EveSong along on this minor expedition. No humans, no Wyrm. The mantra of the Red Talons was of questionable veracity, at best. It was true that the ravages of the Wyrm often followed the course of human immigration, as did the spirit-deadening creep of the Weaver. In nights bygone, EveSong and Evert had debated the inherent causal relationships: Were humans the agents of corruption, or its victims? Like the chicken and egg question, they had never reached a satisfactory conclusion, but their far-ranging philosophical and cosmological ponderings had bound the sept together. Galia had on occasion joined the fray and, like those of her tribe, had displayed an innate understanding of and reverence for all things spiritual. Under the direction of her and Evert, both

Theurges of notable renown, the Sept of the Wailing Glade should have prospered far into the future.

But somewhere along the line they'd gotten off track. The ties of kinship and camaraderie that had united them grew frayed. EveSong blamed Hunch, the metis cub whose birth was an offense to Gaia. Better if they had drowned the cub at birth. But Galia would not have it, and the curse of the metis, like a slow insidious rot, had set in.

Everything is dying. That was what Hunch had said.

"Bah," EveSong muttered to himself. What could that drunken fool know? These might not be the best times the sept had seen, but as soon as Cloudkill recovered from his grief and regained his wherewithal, then everything would change for the better. Over the years, Evert had proven his wisdom and foresight. Generally he exhorted sept members to stay away from areas of heavy human traffic. Many altercations were avoided that way, the Garou safeguarding the caern by not drawing attention to themselves. The proscription was not absolute: EveSong had his bar, and Frederich his strikes against isolated farms; Hunch wandered into town on occasion.

But wait, EveSong caught himself. Hunch was no longer part of the equation. Exile. Outcast. Probably with him gone, the sept's fortunes would change.

For quite a while now, the members of the sept gathered together only rarely; they tolerated one another rather than rejoicing in their kinship. No new Garou came to the sept, or were born to lupus or homid. It was as if the metis' birth had poisoned the well, and Gaia would surrender no more of her warriors to this world. Then brothers of the glade left for elsewhere, or like First Claw and Kelly Fleetfoot ventured far into the Umbra never to return. Yes, they would all be better off without Hunch.

Though it was too late for Galia Rainchild, so long ill, and now three nights dead. Hers had been a grace and beauty

EveSong had never seen matched. The thought that she might still be with them were it not for the birth of malformed Hunch galled him to no end. EveSong wasn't sure exactly how it had happened, but surely Hunch's presence in her belly had caused an infection, of spirit if not of body, and slowly she had wasted away, none realizing her plight until it was too late. If only they could all sit and talk like they had in the old days. It would do Evert so much good; it would do all of them good.

Instead, EveSong was left with *no humans, no Wyrm*, as the height of intellectual stimulation. He was relatively surprised that Shreds Birch had asked him along on the hunt. Perhaps she felt Galia's absence as keenly as Evert did—as EveSong did. Perhaps it was remotely possible that some small good could come of Galia's passing. Would that not honor her life if, through her death, the survivors came closer together? Was that the spark of meaning to be found amidst the darkness?

As he had for the past three days, EveSong searched his memory, reciting to himself stories, songs, lays, of loss and despair. The Garou were a race given to despair, but for them to have survived so long, there must also be an equal measure of hope.

EveSong found little hope in Frederich Night Terror's reaction to the Galliard's accompanying the hunting pack. "Just stay out of the way," Night Terror had snarled.

EveSong had bit his tongue rather than pointing out that a jaunt to kill cows in Farmer Davidson's fields hardly seemed the type of enterprise in which his presence might endanger anyone. Night Terror was not a stoic recipient of sarcasm. Not even beef cows, but *dairy* cows, EveSong had wanted to taunt the Alpha of the pack, but luckily prudence had held sway.

They chose the early morning, when the herd would be turned loose in the fields. EveSong followed behind the others, moving as quietly as he could. He'd be damned if he was going to give Night Terror reason to criticize. Shreds Birch was in good spirits, for she viewed the farm as an invasion of territory that rightfully should be free of humans. Cynthia Slack Ear was happy because her most intimate friend, Shreds Birch, was happy. Night Terror was anticipating the chance to kill, for truly there would be no hunt, no sport, merely the slaughter of a few stupid beasts.

Many years ago, Davidson's farm had been a family affair, small human dwelling, red barn, chicken coop, garden. No longer. The farmhouse had been torn down and replaced by a doublewide trailer, which seemed as much office as dwelling. The chicken coop and garden were gone, as was any attempt at self-sufficiency. The farm, though still in the Davidson family, was now a corporate concern focusing purely on dairy stock that were milked in the sprawling metal building that had replaced the picturesque barn. Several months ago, Night Terror had broken into the "milking facility," where he'd destroyed equipment and several head of cattle—all to spite the humans. Shreds Birch had been after him ever since to revisit the scene and cut a bloody swath on a grander scale. Perhaps that was why Night Terror had not objected more strenuously to EveSong coming along. Destruction bore a spirit all its own, divorced from glory and honor; perhaps there would be a story in the cold morning, after all.

Night Terror led the other three Garou out of the forest and down a sweeping slope toward the metal building. The milk cows, their udders just unhooked from the milking machines, were filing obediently out a bay door on the far side; they did not hear, smell, or see the approach of the attackers. Death caught the pitiful beasts unaware.

The smell of the place sickened EveSong: all machinery and grease and too much manure concentrated in one place. In a moment there was the scent of blood spilling onto hard-packed mud, as Night Terror, rounding the building, ripped the throats from the two closest animals. From the fury of the attack,

EveSong could guess that the Alpha planned to see all fifty or sixty head dead. Humans be damned. Whoever was unlucky enough to be manning the machines this morning would flee — to be found cowering in a cold ditch and muttering incomprehensibly a few hours hence.

Shreds Birch was not far behind Night Terror, and Cynthia Slack Ear bloodied her claws as well. The closest of the bovines began to low apprehensively, but the senses of the domestics were not sharp, and more and more filed ignorantly from the building.

EveSong, the nostrils of his rage-form pricked by the increasing amount of blood spread across the field, hung back nonetheless. He was not piqued at the humans as were the hunting pack. He was distracted by thoughts of departed Galia, of Balthazar who'd stolen away in the night to return her body to her tribe, of Hunch who'd said that the land was dying — Hunch whose fault everything was.

But the scene at hand was compelling. EveSong felt his mouth watering, warm saliva dripping from the bottom of his snout as he watched Night Terror disembowel another helpless beast and gobble the creature's innards with a hunger born of rage. Night Terror, EveSong saw, might not stop with the cattle; he might destroy the entire farm if unchecked. *That* would be a feat worthy of a story; *that* would leave the humans in the area whispering fearfully of these forests for generations to come. Therein Night Terror might find renown.

Within but a few minutes, the hunters had worked their way through perhaps a third of the herd. The field was littered with mangled corpses, yet one after another of the stupid beasts kept turning the corner of the building, each following the tail of her sister before her. EveSong found himself grudgingly respectful of Night Terror's audacity. No picking off of one or two on the outskirts of the grazing herd for him. They would all have fallen in short order—but the hunters were not left to continue the carnage unopposed.

With a great clatter, another bay door, this one facing the field of slaughter, rolled upward, and from within the building stepped a human. He was strangely attired, not as a farmer, but wearing a helmet with a reflective plate that covered his face, and body armor. He held a weapon, some type of heavy gun with which EveSong was not familiar. A second human stepped into the cold, blood-drenched morning, and a third, and a fourth, and a fifth. They raised their weapons as one and fired.

Night Terror, who was closest, saw them: He looked up from his gluttony, ragged strings of gore hanging from his snout, but his eyes, instead of flashing the fire of hunt-frenzy rage, were glassy, his gaze distant and vacant. The shots from the humans slammed into him and knocked him backward off his feet. They were not normal bullets, EveSong could see, but some sort of explosive charge, each detonating as it struck and tearing through his body leaving fist-sized exit holes.

EveSong abandoned his observer's perch at once and charged down the slope as his kin had a few moments before. Shreds Birch and Cynthia heard the shots and were aware of the danger—but they, like Frederich, reacted slowly and clumsily, not as befitting practiced warriors.

Night Terror, his gaping wounds healing over in seconds, climbed back to his feet. He staggered forward only to be met by another explosive salvo that sent him sprawling in the mud and manure.

EveSong charged furiously. Why weren't these humans fleeing? How could they stand and fight? There was no time for contemplation. Pure unfettered fury clouded his vision. The humans fired another volley at Night Terror before he could regain his feet, then they turned and divided their fire among the other three Garou.

Shreds Birch and Cynthia attacked sluggishly. The humans found their targets and the Garou were knocked back by the blasts. EveSong, not yet so close, had better opportunity to dodge, but his rage carried him forward heedless of danger. A shell struck his knee and exploded. He crashed to the ground, crippled. But within moments he was back on his feet, flesh, tendon, muscle re-knit, bone whole and strong.

The humans took advantage of the break in the onslaught to pour fire again at Night Terror. Their laser sights picked out portions of his body that then exploded into huge jagged craters. The stink of smoldering fur joined that of blood and manure. Still Night Terror staggered forward, picking himself off the ground just in time for the next salvo. His wounds healed over only to be opened again the next second. His body was torn asunder to heal itself to be torn asunder again.

Cynthia and Shreds Birch were of little use. They were unsteady; they regained their feet too slowly after each shot to cover any ground. The humans must have lost track of EveSong, however. At a full gallop, he circled wide to the side opposite the others. The humans couldn't concentrate their fire. And with a leap that caught them off guard, he covered the last several dozen yards, landing on the closest enemy.

EveSong grabbed at the gun and the human fired. The explosion, at point-blank range, sent them both to the ground. EveSong, heedless of the blood spewing from the hole in his stomach, was on his feet first. More quickly than any of the others could react, he raked the human's chest, snatched away the fresh corpse's weapon, and turned it on the others. His first shot blew apart three of them. And unlike the Garou, the humans did not get back up.

The remaining human, seeing the odds turned suddenly very much against him, turned and ran. To no effect. EveSong threw down the weapon in disgust and launched himself after the fleeing prey. The body armor proved of little use. Within seconds EveSong had ripped off the helmet and stuffed the human's screaming mouth full of his own internal organs.

His blood up from battle, EveSong found another human, a young man unarmored, pathetic, insane with terror, cowering in a corner of the metal building. The Galliard ripped his head off with one fell slash.

Only after that did EveSong begin to calm. Only then did he return to Shreds Birch and Cynthia, both dazed and unsteady on their feet. Only then did he discover the unmoving body of Night Terror, riddled with gaping holes. But no longer were the wounds healing. Night Terror gazed slack-jawed at the rising sun. There would be a song of this morning's exploits, after all, though not a song that EveSong ever would have expected. A mournful howl. A Dirge for the Fallen.

Chapter 15

"Why in the world does anybody want to keep track of all their garbage?" Kaitlin asked as she made her way through another of the seemingly endless piles of forms and invoices awaiting her attention.

"Darling, it's not money that makes the world go round, and it's not love," Frances said. "It's paperwork."

"But all we do is burn garbage," Kaitlin insisted. On this, just her second day on the job, she already felt like a part of *we*; she was comfortable working with Frances—that was a novel sensation. Like Floyd, Frances seemed genuinely pleasant, not distrustful of Kaitlin because she was black or from a different part of the state. They seemed willing to look out for her—and happy to do so. Like family.

"Well, two reasons," Frances explained. "First, you've got AgriTech, Multinational Corporation. Corporate types, the suits who make all the money while you and I work for closer to minimum, they like paperwork. They like everything in triplicate. They like pink and yellow copies. They're lawyers and accountants. The more paper they create and circulate, the more important they figure they must be, and the more salary they can demand.

"Second, the incinerator is a joint public-private venture. You've got your local government involved, you've got your state government, your feds, you've got the EPA. Everything I said about the corporate types—goes double for the government, maybe triple. The paper trail runs downhill, and at the bottom of that hill, that's where you and I come into the picture. To pick up the mess, make sense out of it, and file it all away."

Kaitlin held up one sheet. "Where does this one go?"

"Let me see…. That's one of our logs of the incoming deliveries. Not stamped yet, so it still has to be confirmed against the invoice from the particular landfill, Roscommon County. So it goes in that filing cabinet, second drawer down. If it were already stamped, it would get photocopied and filed in the third drawer."

"And the copy?"

"Stapled to the blue copy of the landfill invoice. Then it goes to Floyd."

"Why isn't our form on the pressure-sensitive paper like the landfill form? We need copies of both, right?"

Frances guffawed and almost choked on her coffee. "Darling, count your blessings. It could be carbon paper. We have enough carbon paper forms to last us fifteen years, and nothing this side of the incinerator is as bad for a manicure as carbon paper. Your form there is newer, but somebody ordered the wrong type, so we don't have pressure-sensitive. We make photocopies instead. When that batch runs out, we'll get the pressure-sensitive."

"Oh. Well, how much of the wrong form do we have?"

"Um…we're probably down to about 250,000 now. A few more years should do it."

"Oh." Losing herself in the tedious minutiae of the various—literally hundreds of—different forms was simple enough. Kaitlin didn't have to think about anything beyond which drawer and which letter of the alphabet; she didn't have to think about Rindle— What the hell kind of name was that anyway? She needed to ask him sometime. Or maybe she shouldn't push her luck with somebody who casually admitted killing people. Could he have been serious? *Of course* he was serious. She had seen—

But what she had seen didn't hold as much weight here in the daytime, away from him. It was all a bad flashback. It couldn't be real; it sure as hell wasn't part of the normal world, and that was where she wanted to be. That was where Floyd and Frances lived their lives; that was where people had jobs and got paychecks, even minimum wage paychecks; that was where people had food in their kitchens and didn't spend days hiding under a quilt, stoned off their gourd because they were too scared of what they might see otherwise.

If only she could convince herself of that when she was standing in her own house, alone except for a man she thought she'd seen spooling out someone's entrails with his teeth. If only she could convince herself that she hadn't seen any of that when she felt cold sweat run down her side, and a hungry predator's eyes sized her up for the best cut of meat. It was all in her mind, she told herself, time and time again. But only in the daylight, away from him, could she come close to believing.

"Problem?" Frances asked, noticing that Kaitlin was staring blankly at the next form on the stack. "Is that a new one for you? We have about a million different forms, so don't expect to learn them all in the first day or two or ten."

"No, that's okay," Kaitlin said, embarrassed. "I know this one. I just got lost for a second." She smiled sheepishly. The last thing she wanted to do was give Frances the wrong impression—or maybe it would be the *right* impression, but a bad one: that Kaitlin was a pothead who couldn't be trusted, and who hadn't held down a steady job for...well, ever. "Is Floyd...I mean, is Mr. Robesin coming in today or he is off?"

Frances laughed. "You can call him Floyd," she said. "We're not big on formality, and besides, if you call him Mr. Robesin, then you'll want to call me Mrs. Oliver, and that would make me feel like your grandmother and all my hair would turn grey—or the rest of it would. And I think he'll be in, but I'm not sure. There was a message on the answering machine this morning from late last night. He said he'd be out this morning, probably in later, some time this afternoon. Didn't say what for."

"Oh. Okay," Kaitlin said with a half-shrug, and commenced with the filing. She'd asked about his whereabouts, more than anything, merely to change the subject, to shift attention from her own lack of concentration.

"Whenever he shows up," Frances said conspiratorially, "you watch—he'll apologize for being late. Never mind that he's the boss, he'll apologize."

Kaitlin soon found her thoughts drifting again. Now that the image of Rindle's ferocious, man-eating visage had worked its way into her mind, filing wasn't proving enough of a distraction to block it out. Talking with Frances was better, but Kaitlin didn't want to come across as too chatty either, a good-for-nothing. So she tried to keep the questions work oriented. "Why AgriTech," she asked. "I mean, 'Agri' is for agriculture, right? But we're burning garbage. What's that got to do with agriculture? Just because it's keeping the environment safe in general?"

"That, too," Frances said, "but the company works in a lot of different fields. We've developed a lot of different hybrid feeds. You know, for livestock. Healthier for them. Same general kind of thing scientists and farmers have been doing for years and years, but now everybody gets all bent out of shape about genetic engineering. If people only knew half of what they ate…"

That was something that Kaitlin was just as happy not thinking about in too much detail. She was lucky that within just a few minutes, Floyd strolled into the office. He was whistling. Kaitlin had never actually met someone who whistled while he walked merrily along. The habit made her think of him as one of the Seven Dwarfs. Happy? Doc? On occasion, maybe Bashful?

"Good morning, Frances. Good morning, Kaitlin. Sorry about being late. Parent-teacher conferences. I'd forgotten all about them until..." He paused when Kaitlin started laughing. "What? Did I say something? Parent-teacher conferences? What?"

"Are your ears burning?" Frances asked him. "We were just talking about you."

"Oh. Okay." He seemed relieved that he hadn't left his pants unzipped or something like that. "Well, then..."

"Is that for us?" Frances asked, indicating a handful of papers that he was carrying.

"Hm? Oh, yes. I ran into Larry on the way in—Larry Evans," he said to Kaitlin. "Dr. Evans. He's the administrator for the lab. Here." He handed the forms to Frances.

She flipped through them and seemed mildly surprised. "Five transfers all at once. That's odd isn't it?"

Floyd shrugged. "Well, Larry's a strange fellow. They must have finished up a project."

"Aren't you in charge?" Kaitlin asked, then realized the question sounded pejorative, which she didn't mean for it to. "I mean, you're the director. He works for you...right?"

Floyd chuckled. "The lab is part of the R&D branch of the company. We handle some of the administrative aspects of their operation, but functionally I'd say they're semi-autonomous."

"Which means," Frances added, "that the bigwigs think that anybody on this side of that barbed wire might be a corporate spy, so they don't tell us anything about what they're doing."

Floyd gave Frances a look that seemed to say *don't you go starting rumors.* "That's not completely true," he said. "I was telling Kaitlin about some of the scrubbing and reclamation techniques yesterday. Fact is, I wouldn't understand most of the hard science even if they did want to hand that information out. So we just keep the plant running."

Frances, behind Floyd, nodded and winked at Kaitlin. "Yes, sir, Mr. Robesin," Frances said. This seemed to exasperated Floyd to no end, and as he sighed and headed for his office, the two women laughed quietly.

Floyd stopped and turned back to Kaitlin. "Oh, I almost forgot," he said, tapping himself with a finger on the side of his head. "Kaitlin, I mentioned to Anne, my wife that you'd started work, and she was hoping you'd be able to come over for dinner. Do you have plans for Friday?"

For an instant, Kaitlin panicked, and immediately she was embarrassed for reacting that way for no good reason. "Friday. That's tomorrow."

Floyd thought about that for a moment. "Yes. I guess you're right. If you already have plans, or if some other time—"

"No, tomorrow would be fine," she said too quickly, trying to cover her agitation but just making it more obvious. Why was Floyd doing this? Did his wife like to check out the new help, make sure the new office girl wasn't too pretty?

"Great," Floyd said, trying to sound pleasant and enthusiastic, but managing little more than befuddled. "Um...I can take you from here...tomorrow, that is. And drive you home afterward. I mean...you don't have a car do you?"

"No, I don't," she said, forcing herself to remain calm. "That would be fine...very nice of you."

"Great," he said again, and then slipped away into his office.

"You'll like Anne," Frances said reassuringly. "She's a real doll. You'll like her."

Kaitlin smiled and nodded, and then tried to lose herself again in the filing.

Black Rindle raised his head. He stretched his complaining bones and stood from the worn, dirty blanket that had come to be his sole comfort. *It has become your kennel,* said a voice, low, vitriolic, seductive. *She keeps you like a dog.*

He looked slowly around, eyes narrowed, but there was no one to have spoken the words, only the same stark room with the quilt heaped on the bed much like the blanket on the floor. The walls were bare aside from their cracked and peeling paint. Water stains stretched across the ceiling, visible signs of an unseen threat that, if unchecked, would over time rot away more and more wood and plaster until, in the end, the structure was uninhabitable. In the windows Black Rindle saw his own distorted reflection, and beyond the wavering glass only darkness, impenetrable black night.

Had he slept so long? He didn't think so. Kaitlin should be home from her job, but he didn't hear her. Pausing and listening a moment longer, he heard...nothing. Absolutely nothing. *You hear nothing, see nothing, do nothing. Worthless metis lapdog,* said the voice.

Black Rindle stepped from the bedroom and his Homid feet were now paws of his wolf-form. On all fours, he found himself not in the upstairs hallway, but in the deep forest, the sky as black as the windows had been, a tranquil ocean unmarred by the crude reflection of a deformed mockery. He started along the path that opened before him, drawn inexorably forward, trotting at first, and then running, his wolf senses missing no detail of the great wood around him: sight of tiny Lizard wriggling across the trail; earthy aroma of fallen leaves, packed layer upon layer, decaying from the bottom; creak of restless boughs. *This is where you belong,* said the voice. *Alone in the wilderness. Slave to no human. Seen by no Garou.*

Black Rindle could hear reason in the words. In absence, he would not remind the others of his kind of the disfavor of Gaia courted by his creation, and they would be unable to heap abuse upon him. As for humans, he'd had no use for them for most of his life. He would be better off, happier, off by himself. They all would be better off.

"Would you stay here, then?" the other wolf asked.

The forest path was gone. Black Rindle stood in a secluded dell, a vivacious spring bubbling and filling a depression in the near end, and seated beside the pool the horrendously ugly wolf who Black Rindle knew as Meneghwo.

"I would stay," Black Rindle said sharply, "if I thought I could be alone."

Meneghwo pondered this; he seemed eventually to comprehend the inherent suggestion. "Do not worry," he said, mild in tone and manner. "I will not stay long. This is your dreamworld, not mine."

Dreamworld. Black Rindle glanced around again. "Then none of this is real?"

"As real as you want or need it to be," Meneghwo said. "You would stay here?" he asked again. "You would leave behind your sept, your family, your human?"

She is not a simple human, said the reemergent voice. *She is dangerous. She sees us. She is Wyrm-tainted.*

"I have no family. I have no sept," Black Rindle snapped. "Why don't you leave me alone, and we'll all be happy."

"I did not come to your dream in search of you," Meneghwo said. "You came in search of me."

The spirit-wolf lies. He would have you suffer further. He won't even leave you to dream in peace. None of the others want you back.

Meneghwo scowled. "I think that is enough of that," he said. Suddenly he was a great Crinos beast coming toward Black Rindle.

Black Rindle grew fearful but, as in the worst of his nightmares, he was unable to move. His feet were rooted to the ground. Feet. He wore his man-form once again. His body assumed shapes at capricious whim, not by conscious choice.

Very little of the conscious was tenacious enough to hold sway in the dreamworld.

Meneghwo raised a clawed hand—but did not strike. Instead, he laid his hand on Black Rindle's chest, on what Black Rindle saw there to his own amazement: a second mouth. The mouth grimaced in anger and frustration. *He is not thinking of you, only of himself,* the mouth said. *He is stupid and ugly, and he would have you share his fate. Pathetic, stupid creature—!* The last words, a harsh, shrill screech, ended abruptly as the mouth closed. And then was gone, as if it had never been.

Black Rindle listened to the silence, unbroken except for the burbling of the spring.

Meneghwo patted him again on his chest, then turned away, once again a giant wolf, and Black Rindle was wolf as well. "So you would stay," the patchwork wolf said, shaking his head. "So much like your father."

"I have no father," Black Rindle said, still staring in wonder at his own chest.

"Do you remember the words which Owl spoke to you?" Meneghwo asked.

Black Rindle nodded. "He said that rage and hatred are not the same."

"And...?" Meneghwo prompted.

"That I must rely upon rage without surrendering to hatred."

"Then why do you ignore him?" Meneghwo spoke these, his first sharp words, but then continued more kindly. "Are you so much wiser than Owl?"

"I...I..." Black Rindle sputtered, unable to respond until his anger flared and gave him voice. "I am to hatred what the open desert is to the blazing, afternoon sun. When the burning ceases, I will look kindly upon the sun. But will this come to pass before the end of time?"

"So much like your father," Meneghwo said again, more sad than piqued. "Do you not see that Owl is gone? None remain who are worthy of him, so how can he ward off the sickness of the land? And Water Snake, too. Now that Galia is dead, he has no reason to stay."

Black Rindle had *not* known that the spirits had fled entirely, but his pride was pricked by accusations of ignorance. "I know that the land is sick, but I know too that no one will listen to me, the accursed of Gaia. What am I alone supposed to do?"

"Are resentment and bitterness so different from hatred?" the patchwork wolf asked.

"You are ugly and stupid," Black Rindle snapped. "Far more accursed that I am." He fought the temptation to glance down at his chest, so familiar did his words sound in his ears.

"So much like your father," Meneghwo said a third time, as he might the words of ritual. "You would dwell here amidst what is not, while the worlds crumble around you. But always the fault lies elsewhere. Could you not entice Owl to return?"

"You are a fool! An idiot!" Black Rindle snarled at the much larger wolf. "If this is my dreamworld, then leave me."

"As the mundane world is to heart and the Umbra is to spirit, this place is to psyche," Meneghwo said. "Neglect any at your peril."

"Away!" Black Rindle shouted. "Leave me!"

The great patchwork wolf stared nonplussed at Black Rindle for long moment, then lowered his head. The next instant, he was gone—as was the forest, the dell, the spring. Black Rindle stood amidst a vast, featureless desert, the merciless sun baking him along with the hard, cracked earth.

Black Rindle awoke upon his blanket. Kaitlin's blanket. In Kaitlin's bedroom, in Kaitlin's house. The sun was not quite set. His mouth and throat were parched, yet he could not for the longest time summon the energy to raise his complaining bones from the floor. Instead, he lay silently and stared at the water stains on the ceiling, visible signs of an unseen threat.

Chapter 16

"You stink," Black Rindle said, almost before Kaitlin had pulled the front door closed behind her. He confronted her in the front hall.

"Thanks. Nice to see you too," she said.

He winced at the edge in her voice. It seemed that since the first time he'd laid eyes on her, she'd been constantly either afraid of him or angry at him. He wasn't trying to insult her, but never in his life had he been anything but plainspoken. He'd never done well at treading lightly where someone else's feelings were involved—never before had he been inclined to try.

"Not normal...human stink," he tried to explain.

"Oh, so now I don't even stink like a human. What do I stink like, a groundhog?"

"Wyrm."

"I stink like a worm. Great. You know, I don't expect, 'Hi, honey. How was your day at work.' I don't know *what* I expect. But not this."

"You have to take me there," he said.

"*What?*"

"To the place you work."

"The incinerator?"

"Yes."

"I just got *back* from there. I'm not turning around and—"

"Later, then. But tonight," he added urgently. "When no one is there."

"I am *not* walking all the way—"

"I'll carry you."

"*What?*"

Black Rindle began to pace up and down the hallway. He tried not to scrunch his hands into fists and snarl at her, but Kaitlin's resistance was infuriating. He couldn't *tell* her. There was no way he could explain what was happening. Why couldn't she just agree to what he said? She was watching him. Very closely. He could feel her wary gaze tracing his every move. Fear and resentment—those were the only lenses through which she ever looked at him. One or the other, sometimes both. And Black Rindle hated that. He pressed his forehead against the wall and groaned in frustration. Kaitlin slipped past him to the kitchen.

After taking a deep breath, he followed her and tried to keep in mind his plan, which was in danger of being lost to his agitation. She had reacted in ignorance when he'd mention the Wyrm: further proof that the girl was not a spirit creature, as he'd so fancifully speculated, and that she wasn't a minion of corruption. Or perhaps she was merely skillful enough to deceive him, to draw him in.

He waited and calmed himself while she rooted around in the cupboard. Was the Wyrm-stench stronger than yesterday? he wondered. Or were his suspicions playing tricks with his senses? When she had settled on a banana and a granola bar and taken a seat at the card table, he took another deep breath and tried again, speaking slowly, methodically, almost painfully: "Kaitlin, I can't explain...I mean...you...you have to stop going to that place." He blurted that out and, as the scowl contorted Kaitlin's face, he began smashing his fist against the wall. "Damn! Damn! Damn!"

After a moment, he caught himself, regained control, stopped his cocked fist from striking the wall yet again. Kaitlin's scowl had changed to wide-eyed alarm, which was equally as aggravating to Black Rindle. It seemed to be the dynamic of their relationship: She went out into the human world and came back all haughty and scornful. He got angry and scared the daylights out of her. Black Rindle didn't want to be angry at her; he didn't want to frighten her. He looked at Kaitlin and her fear wounded him.

"I'm not ordering you," he said apologetically, after the long, drawn-out silence. "I want to convince you, to show you. So you can make up your own mind." So many years had passed since Black Rindle had cared what anyone thought about him. To be angry, to lash out, that was his normal way, ingrained by relentless repetition. Even in his dream, he'd lashed out against Meneghwo, who for the second time had been trying to help him.

Kaitlin, too, had tried to help him. And this badgering was how he rewarded her? She was watching him still, her banana peeled but ignored. No wonder she distrusted and feared him. He'd never given her reason to regard him any other way. Maddeningly, though, that was what he was *trying* to do now: prove to her that he was looking out for her best interests, keep her from harm. And she wouldn't let him! He was attempting to heed Meneghwo's admonitions, to some degree, at least. Black Rindle might not be able to bring himself to forgive his former septmates; he might not be able to care about the fates of the Garou world or the human world, which both had rejected and despised him for so long. But this girl had tried to help him, and in some strange way she seemed as caught between worlds as he was.

"Kaitlin, I...you..." He was brought up short by her skeptical expression. Words and snarls tangled in this throat. Calm fled. With great effort, he restrained an explosion of fury and invective. How could one young woman prove so difficult to help? Black Rindle closed his eyes, and with a great sigh swallowed his fire.

"You know," Kaitlin said tentatively, still somewhat cowed by his histrionics, "you're not the easiest person in the world to help. I mean…well, I'm not a shrink or anything, and I'm not coming from the most normal of situations myself, but I…I just don't understand where you're coming from. I don't think I can. And you probably can't understand where *I'm* coming from. It's like we're both coming from these really weird places…I mean *really* weird…but they're both completely different, just not…normal. You know? And you…I mean, your friends beat you up and leave you to freeze to death in the woods, and… Well, your *name*, for Christ's sake. People call you Blackie Hunchback? That's gotta leave some scars. And your real name's not much better. Black Rindle. What kind of…I mean, what the hell was your mother thinking?"

"My mother died three nights ago," Black Rindle said, staring at the dingy linoleum. "The night before you found me."

Kaitlin's mouth hung open just a little. She said nothing for a long moment, then: "Oh. I…I'm sorry. I…I didn't mean…I don't know what to say."

Black Rindle looked up at her. "Say you'll go with me tonight," he pressed. "I can find the incinerator without you. I know the area. We weren't supposed to…we just never went near it. I need to find out what's there…and show you."

"'We'? Who's 'we'?" she asked.

"Say that you'll go with me."

"Tell me who 'we' is. Your friends? The friends who beat the hell out of you? Those friends? You don't like to talk about them."

"No, I don't. And, yes, my former friends. If you're lucky, you'll never meet them."

"If *they're* lucky," she said, biting off the tip of the banana fairly savagely. "I'd have to tell them a thing or two."

"You'll go, then," Black Rindle said.

Kaitlin folded her arms, chewed the banana, and glared at him.

They set out several hours after dark. Black Rindle offered again to carry Kaitlin if she didn't want to walk that far, but she refused. He suspected that she didn't think he could do it. Understandable: He walked with a limp and his hump would not have made for a comfortable piggy-back ride. But she was so small it would have been no problem, even in his man-form.

The Tap House, as they passed, was deserted. A piece of plywood was nailed over the broken pane of glass on the door. Black Rindle toyed with the idea of breaking in again and grabbing a bottle. He hadn't had a drink in over twenty-four hours, not since he'd finished Kaitlin's ceremonial beer. The sensation of prolonged sobriety—twenty-four hours at a time being prolonged—was not completely, or even predominately, pleasant. There was too much he didn't want to think about. If he'd been drunk all night and all day, he wouldn't have been thinking about Galia; he wouldn't have been thinking about and hating Evert, or about what Balthazar had said: that the land was dying. He wouldn't have cared so much that Kaitlin came home smelling of the Wyrm—

Not true, he realized. He would have been thinking about all of those things regardless; he just wouldn't have felt compelled, or perhaps able, to do anything about any of them.

The incinerator complex was almost five miles away from Kaitlin's house. Black Rindle was deceptively strong and fast; he was used to being underestimated because of his hunch and limp. Quite often on the way, he had to stop and let Kaitlin catch up. She was doing her best, there was just no way her short legs were going to keep up with him. The closer the two got to the complex, the slower Black Rindle proceeded and the more easily Kaitlin kept pace. The last mile they hiked in silence. The girl started to speak at one point, and Black Rindle shushed her—which made her more than a bit angry. But she held her tongue.

They followed the road until the last curve. Once the complex was in sight, Black Rindle led Kaitlin into the forest. The main gate would be locked at this hour; that was certain. So Black Rindle rushed ahead the last hundred yards. By the time Kaitlin, cursing under her breath, caught up with him at the fence line, Black Rindle was wearing his man-form once again and, in a very self-satisfied way, pointing out a low tear in the chain link just large enough for a person to crawl through.

"What?" Kaitlin whispered. "So you found a hole in the fence. Big deal." He started to shush her again, but she jabbed a finger in his chest and whispered emphatically: "And don't you run off and leave me again!"

She followed him through the fence. The trees thinned quickly on the inside, so the two intruders kept to the edges of the compound, hidden among the shadows as much as possible. Black Rindle began to sniff at the air. He could sense more clearly now the taint of Wyrm that he'd noticed clinging to Kaitlin. His elders, on more than one occasion, had told him that it was not a true scent he was picking up; it wasn't his nose but his soul that could track down Wyrm-taint. Black Rindle had always been dubious—it sure smelled like a real scent to him—and he had earned the rebukes of his elders by voicing his skepticism.

"Why do you always do that?" Kaitlin whispered, but she asked in a way that suggested she knew the answer—but wanted to be wrong.

"Show me where you work," he said in the hushed tones they had both adopted.

"If you just wanted a tour, we could have come tomorrow," she said.

"Show me."

They crept forward. A few floodlights illuminated portions of the gravel road that ran through the central portion of the compound. Black Rindle and Kaitlin made their way along the rear of one of the metal warehouses. At the corner, they stopped and Kaitlin pointed across the road.

"That one. There," she said, indicating a small brick building.

Black Rindle was doubtful—not that she worked there, but that the building was what he was looking for. The disturbing whiff of Wyrm-taint seemed to cling to everything in the area. Why, he wondered, had Evert Cloudkill never had the sept investigate this place and take whatever action was necessary? The alpha had always ordered them to give the complex a wide berth.

"What else is here?" Black Rindle asked her.

Kaitlin counted of on her fingers: "The incinerator, the lab, and the cinderblock thing."

"The what?"

"I forget what they call it. Where they make cinderblocks. The reclamation thingy."

"Show me."

They worked their way back to the fence line and then headed deeper into the compound, keeping to the perimeter and the protection of the trees and deepest shadows. After a few hundred yards, they moved back toward the gravel road and found themselves near the rear of a second brick building, much larger than the first, and surrounded by another barbed-wire topped chain-link fence.

Kaitlin seemed confused by the scene, which undoubtedly appeared quite different to her consumed as it was by the vagaries of night. "I didn't think we'd come this far," she said, "but this is the lab.

There were no windows on the building, and no way to tell from the rear if it was occupied. "Wait here," Black Rindle whispered.

"What?"

"I'll be right back," he assured her. He was not at his stealthiest in man-form, but he made less noise moving half-crouched toward the front of the building by himself than the two of them would have. Sneaking as close as he dared, he saw that the gate in front of the building was locked. Lights were on inside, and three sedans were parked near the building within the fenced area, but Black Rindle could discern no movement or evidence beyond the number of cars that might have given away how many people were inside. He could, however, sense more keenly the taint of the Wyrm here, deeper in the compound, than he had closer to the state road, near Kaitlin's office.

"Let's keep going," he whispered to Kaitlin when he'd rejoined her.

The fence around the lab did not extend all the way back to the perimeter fence. In fact, the lab fence joined the back corner of the building; there were no rear entrances or exits to be protected, only a steep bank that fell away into a gully behind the lab. Black Rindle had his mind on the incinerator proper and the reclamation "thingy" as he and Kaitlin descended into the gully so that they could climb up the other side and bypass the lab without cutting through the lighted areas to the front. He kept an eye on the girl; she was light and agile and handled the climb well. Increasingly, as they made their way down the darkened slope, Black Rindle caught wind of Wyrm-stench. He thought at first it was a trick of the wind, but there was no wind in the murky hollow—just a brackish trickle of water in the lowest recesses of the ditch.

Black Rindle had a better nose for Wyrm-taint than did some Garou, than did *many* Garou. He'd always suspected that was why the elders resented him—that, and his habitual recalcitrance. As he climbed down the last few steps to the base of the gully, the stench grew overwhelming. Kaitlin climbed down to stand beside him and seemed to notice nothing amiss. The water was no deeper than the soles of their boots, yet Black Rindle's stomach grew queasy. He fought down his physical repulsion and traced the water to a wide pipe that protruded from the hillside behind the lab and was capped by a thick metal plate—with a tiny hole that allowed the water passage. He pressed one arm over his mouth and nose.

"What?" Kaitlin asked.

Black Rindle found it hard to believe that she couldn't smell the presence of corruption, of decay and malignance. Perhaps she was only human after all. Not some creature of spirit. Maybe there was some other explanation that the Delirium had passed her over and left her whole of mind. "You can't smell it, can you?"

"It's stagnant water," she said, nonplussed by the intensity of his reaction. "It stinks a little. That's what stagnant water does. You're not going to tell me that I smell like that when I come home, because I *don't* come down here and wallow in the ditch. I didn't even know this was back here."

Black Rindle nodded. "This is what I brought you here to see." And then he stepped sideways into the spirit world.

One instant Kaitlin was looking at him, and the next he was gone. It was as if Black Rindle, in mid-stride, had ceased to exist. Kaitlin blinked several times and waited for the optical trick of the night to correct itself, but no matter how hard she peered was rewarded with nothing but empty darkness. Drainage ditch, pipe, hillside, back of the lab—but no Black Rindle.

"Rindle?" she whispered urgently to the night and received no reply. *"Where the hell did you go?"*

And then she heard a voice—not Black Rindle's voice. Two voices. Two men up and out of the ditch, coming closer.

"What did you hear?"

"I told you—somebody talking."

"Why would anybody be here tonight?"

"Why would anybody have been at the farm this morning?"

A beam of light, and then a second, bobbed against the top edge of the gully above Kaitlin's head. The two men were not yet close enough to see down into the bottom. They had stopped talking, but a different sound, the metallic grating of a gun being cocked, made Kaitlin flinch. She crouched down, cowering, alone in the darkness. At first she'd been worried that she might lose her job for trespassing. Now that seemed inconsequential. If AgriTech was as paranoid about industrial spies as Floyd had said, what were they likely to shoot first and ask questions later? What would they think about a scared black girl hiding in a muddy ditch?

The patches of light on the gully wall were moving lower as the men came closer. Kaitlin scrunched down farther, on all fours in the stagnant water, which *did* smell like sludge this close up. But she didn't care. She would have drunk a gallon of the stuff if it meant the guys with the flashlights and guns wouldn't find her. As the lights drew closer, she wondered if maybe she should call out to the men, so that they wouldn't come on her by surprise. Maybe they'd be less likely to shoot her that way.

When Black Rindle tapped Kaitlin on the shoulder, she stifled a loud gasp, as well as the urge to tell him exactly what she thought of him running off and leaving her again. He glanced toward the top of the ditch. The silhouettes of the men's heads were visible against the night sky. The beams of light moved toward the bottom of the ditch, and just as they reached Kaitlin, Black Rindle took her hand and her normal world ceased to exist.

Chapter 17

EveSong found comfort in the closeness of his brethren, though Gaia knew few enough of them remained. Five were all. He could remember the days when they had numbered easily thrice that many. There ought, at least, to be one more, but Evert Cloudkill was nowhere to be seen.

Stretched out upon a bier of resin-soaked timbers, Frederich Night Terror appeared more peaceful, more at rest, than ever he had in life. He was—*had* been, EveSong corrected himself—one of the full moons who reveled less in the hunt, more in the kill; and he had died as he had lived, elbow-deep in gore. EveSong had seen other Garou die, but he would have expected Luna to cease rising in the east before he would have thought to witness Night Terror meet his doom.

The tale-teller of the Sept of the Wailing Glade glanced around once more, thinking that Cloudkill must surely be on hand by now, perhaps lurking in the shadows, coming to grips with the fall of his most renowned warrior. EveSong peered into the deep shadows, but Evert was not to be seen.

The others were present. Not far away stood Claudia Stands Firm, impassive, her expression as stern as a roiling stormcloud, all churning energy, contained but about to unleash its fury. Barks-at-Shadows was more visibly distraught. The moon-calf lay near the bier, his front paws spread before him, chin resting on the ground between them. Every so often, he breathed a plaintive sigh, almost a whimper. His ears lay back on his head.

Shreds Birch and Cynthia Slack Ear kept silent vigil over the fallen. As Frederich's packmates, they had spent most of the day constructing the bier: hardwood logs seeped in pin resin. When the time came, it would light quickly, burn long, hot, and true.

If the time came.

After another glance around the clearing, EveSong skirted the bier and approached Stands Firm. "Where is he?" he asked her, not needing to explain of whom he spoke.

Claudia did not look at up him—she wore her wolf-form—but growled almost under her breath: "He will be here. I am sure he will be here."

"You told him?"

In way of response, she bared her teeth at such a question that didn't bear asking. Was she not the Warder? Of course she had told him.

EveSong surveyed the scene glumly. Five Garou were all that remained of a once-proud sept. Their numbers were dwindling by the day. Galia dead. Balthazar, who was no true member of the sept but a constant figure for many months just the same, gone. Hunch exiled. Night Terror killed. Who, EveSong wondered, would be next? Who else would fall and be denied the appropriate rites? Cloudkill's absence rankled further because they had yet, three days after the fact, to pay Galia proper homage. They had been more than patient, EveSong thought. Evert's grief must be near to unbearable, they all had assumed, and so had not pressed the matter. The alpha would lead them in the rites when he was able, and until that time they would console themselves, each with his or her own private mourning. But tragedy had now struck the sept again. And where was Cloudkill at the appointed hour?

"This must come to an end," EveSong muttered, as he stalked away from Claudia Stands Firm, the bier, and the other mourners.

First EveSong went to the shallow cave, the cramped space where Galia had spent her final weeks growing sicker and weaker, the place where she had died. Balthazar Spirit Walker had watched over her there. He had come to the sept after she had fallen ill and was no longer able to speak to her brethren. The Strider had spoken of a charge entrusted to him by the spirits to watch over her. EveSong and the others had assumed that Spirit Walker brought with him some type of healing. He had never left her side. But Galia Rainchild did not grow stronger, did not recover from her affliction; and when she died, Balthazar had stolen away with her body.

EveSong had been outraged. Evert Cloudkill had said nothing; he'd been morose, as he'd been for months, but he had raised not so much as a growl of anger at the injustice done him, done the sept.

There was a chance, EveSong had thought, that Evert might be at the cave, privately expressing the grief he seemed unable to confront communally. The cave, however, was empty as a forgotten promise, silent as a tomb.

EveSong could not see the place without thinking of Galia, of Evert, of Spirit Walker…and of Hunch. The surly metis had come often to sit with Galia, to watch her unresponsive form through pained eyes, and even to shed tears for her. Hunch, as ardently as any of them, had hoped for a different outcome to her illness. Out of guilt, EveSong reminded himself, lest he grow sentimental over the churl. Too little, too late. No doubt Hunch *had* regretted that his birth had doomed his dam. Better if the freak had never been born. EveSong spat in the dirt and scraped the thick mix with the toe of his boot, trying to eradicate memory of the exile.

Next the Galliard made his way to the lesser fire circle. The soot-blackened pit and the surrounding ring of stones were much smaller than the greater circle, where Frederich's bier would be lit, where Hunch—damn his name for refusing to fade away—had confronted his sire and been cast out of the sept. Cloudkill was not here. EveSong had not expected him to be— but the tale-teller had hoped....

This was the place that three of them—himself, Evert, and Galia—had often sat late into the night and talked, debated, told stories, shared songs, or simply howled greeting to Sister Luna. For Cloudkill to come here might have meant that the alpha was coming to terms with his grief, venting his sorrow, mourning the loss of the past so that he might continue into the future. As far as EveSong knew, Evert had not set foot in this circle since Galia had fallen ill. He had barely spoken a word, in fact. For months he had been a slave of his own heartache—no, the heartache of Galia's passing belonged to them all, yet Cloudkill had taken it on himself, and in so doing had denied the rest of them any part in the anguish that was this portion of the Great Wheel. Worse yet, without the communal acceptance of the loss, until the sept as a whole grieved, the Wheel would not continue to turn and bring the renewal that always follows death.

"Why did you have to leave us?" EveSong spoke to the ring of silent stones, though his words were for Galia. Then he spoke to the absent Cloudkill: "Haven't you had enough time?" Galia's memory deserved better. The sept deserved better. Frederich Night Terror deserved better.

Thought of the fallen Ahroun, of his body which Evert had yet so much as to view, kindled EveSong's rage. Galia was gone. Frederich, now too, was gone. The proper rites must be observed. Prepared or not, Evert had to see this, had to do this. He was alpha. He was crescent moon. It was his place, his duty.

Determination and a rising sense of outrage drove EveSong onward. He turned his face to the west, the direction of the sun sunk beyond the earth, the direction of darkness and endings.

Away from the fire rings, away from the shrines to Owl and Water Snake, away from the dirty cave where Galia had breathed her last, there was a place not to be disturbed; a place where the spirits saw that neither bird nor insect trespassed, nor did the North Wind with its fiercest blowing touch a single leaf of a single tree. This was the place to which they all should have come—after the rites of passing for Galia, after the fire that would claim the broken body of Frederich. This was the place where the Garou of the Sept of the Wailing Glade came all together or none at all. This was the place where EveSong found Evert Cloudkill.

The alpha stood before the Ash Tree. He held himself awkwardly, head cocked to one side, one shoulder higher than the other, as if a painful crick in his neck wouldn't allow him to stand to his full height. Cloudkill's once dark hair was sprinkled through with grey; his face was like leather, exposed for years to sun and rain and cold, wrinkles deeper than EveSong had ever noticed before, worried canyons worn by rivers of tears.

"Evert," said EveSong quietly, hesitant to disturb his alpha, but prompted by the need of the people. Cloudkill did not answer, did not acknowledge his tale-teller, and so EveSong called him again, a bit more forcefully this time: "Evert."

Cloudkill heard this time. Slowly he turned, and in the first glance of those pale green eyes, EveSong saw...nothing.

Nothing and everything.

Gone were the fire and steel of a leader of Garou. Gone were the glimmers of insight, deeper than the broadest and deepest lake. Gone was the surety with which Cloudkill had looked into the hearts of his people, and into his own heart. He was a tired and sorrowful old man, as broken as surely as was Frederich upon his bier.

"Evert," said EveSong again, gently once more, for fear that a harsh word might shatter this man whom the sept needed so desperately.

"She should be here," Cloudkill said, bewildered, disoriented, unable to comprehend the great distance between *what should be* and *what was*.

EveSong, for perhaps the first time in his life, was struck dumb. *She should be here.* Not a statement of regret or anger; rather a lament, a plea. Cloudkill's words seethed with confusion and loss, were raw like a wound infested by maggots.

Harano. EveSong had seen the face of despair in the past, and it stared back at him now in Cloudkill's suffering eyes. It burrowed into the soul and consumed one from within. EveSong staggered, struck by an icy cold blow to his chest that felt as if it cracked his sternum and laid open his heart to the elements. No, this could not be.

"You know about Frederich," EveSong said. Cloudkill couldn't be as bad off as he seemed. He mustn't be. EveSong's responsibility was to pull him back, to remind him of *what was*, of duty and hope. But Cloudkill regarded him with uncomprehending, washed out green eyes. "Claudia told you," Frederich insisted, firmly, gently guiding Evert back to reality. The alpha needed merely time, direction.

"She should be here," Cloudkill said again at last. Doubtfully, he looked back and forth between EveSong and the tree.

The Ash Tree was misnamed in a sense. It was not an ash but an old oak, dead, split, struck many years ago by lightning, its core hollowed out until only the stolid shell remained. The tree was named for and made holy by that which filled its heart: the ashes of the departed, three handfuls scooped from the consumed bier of each Garou passed beyond. Three offerings of each of the dead; the first honored Owl, the second Water Snake, and the third Mother Gaia, who bound them all as one.

She should be here. Galia. Cloudkill recognized only her absence and that it was wrong. But the Wheel could not stop for the sake of hurtful injustice.

"Frederich is waiting," EveSong said gently. "You are alpha. You are crescent moon. He is laid out upon his bier."

"She should be here." Cloudkill's ache, the sound of his enforced solitude, echoed throughout the clearing.

"She is gone, Evert. She was ours in life, but Balthazar has taken her back to her own people in death."

"*Balthazar.*" Mention of the Strider struck through to Cloudkill's rage. "Balthazar Spirit Walker!" he roared defiantly to the heavens, the fire suddenly rekindled in his eyes. "Cursed be the day I allowed you into this caern! Cursed be the day you crawled from your dam's belly! I would tear her apart to keep you from being born!"

EveSong's shock gave way quickly—gave way to *hope.* Where there was rage, there was hope. Perhaps coddling was not the answer. Seeing a chance, he seized upon the alpha's fury: "Then let us track him down and teach him that lesson," EveSong urged Cloudkill. "Teach him with blood, so he will never forget. Galia came here of her own will. She was of our people. The Uktena have claim to her no longer. She should be here, her ashes with us."

Cloudkill's chest heaved as the fury took hold of him. He wore his man-form still, but for how much longer? He scraped his fingers down the sides of his face, leaving bloody tracks where he tore gashes in his own flesh. A wail of loss denied and rekindled rage rose from deep in his belly.

EveSong watched the effect of his urging, and measured his next words with care: "But first let us tend to Frederich."

Cloudkill stiffened as if doused with painfully cold water. His wail, trailing off, ceased at once. He stood with his face buried in his hands, blood dripping between his fingers.

"You are alpha, Evert," said EveSong, trying to reach through to that place between despair and rage, between Harano and carnage. "You are crescent moon, and Frederich is laid out upon his funeral bier." EveSong waited, his hands limber at his sides, ready to match rage-form for rage-form if he had pushed Cloudkill too far, too fast. He watched as Evert trembled so fiercely that surely his coiled muscles must snap.

And then, slowly, the tension drained from Cloudkill's shoulders, his arms, all his body. He lowered his hands, revealing a face streaked with blood and salty tears.

EveSong felt his rage-form calling to him. So close to the precipice had they come, yet still it was uncertain that he would be able to drag Cloudkill out of the black chasm of Harano. But fire there still was, and rage.

"Let us go to Frederich," said EveSong, sweat dripping from his brow despite the cold. A crisp breeze caught him and ran down the back of his neck, making him flinch and shiver. Within the tree, Garou ashes swirled and scraped against the wall of their tomb. Something about the sound struck EveSong as odd, but his attention was absorbed by Cloudkill. The tale-teller reached out a hand and, after a long moment, Evert grasped him in return. "Let us go to Frederich," EveSong said softly. The alpha smiled weakly, and then together, with the wind in their hair, they left that place.

Chapter 18

Kaitlin fell into the coldest lake she had ever felt. The shock tore the breath from her lungs. She gagged and thrashed for a moment before realizing that no water was choking her. She wasn't drowning. Yet her feet could find no purchase. She was blind, from bright light or complete darkness she couldn't tell. Snowblind. Or dead. Flashlights and guns. Patches of light moving down the side of the gully. The sound of guns being cocked. The panic reflex gripped her again. She coughed and flailed at…at what: water, air, darkness?

"Be still," said Rindle's voice, calm, soothing. "Be still for a moment."

He was here, then. Wherever *here* was. She was not alone. "Where are you? Can you see? I can't… I'm blind. Is it just me? Where are you?"

"Be still." He was very close, the words spoken quietly in her ear. She felt his breath on her neck.

She reached out. Her fingertips found substance at last, touched…his body, a shoulder. She buried her fingers in the fabric of his ragged jacket, scrunched it in her fist, held on for dear life. "Did they shoot me? Am I dying?"

"You're not dying. Just be still for a moment. Trust me."

Trust him. In Kaitlin's experience, the only people who ever said "Trust me" were people who couldn't be trusted. She didn't want to trust him; she wanted to *see*.

Slowly, indistinct shapes began to take form. She tried to look around. Where were the men with the flashlights and guns? She wasn't sure. Firm hands grasped either side of her face.

"Be still," Rindle said again, less gently this time. "You ever try listening?"

"Do *you*?" she shot back.

Rindle growled—*literally* growled. Kaitlin tried to jerk away, but his hands were too strong against the sides of her face. She thought for a moment that she saw the wolf's head that had stared back at her the other night, but then she saw that it was just his rough unshaven face and disheveled hair. The face she had grown used to. She was confused, caught between her relief at being able to see, and her relief at seeing *him*.

As her vision gradually expanded and returned to normal, she saw that her relief was premature. Wherever she saw, whatever she saw, nothing was normal.

She and Rindle were not in the gully behind the lab. They were on a small, crumbling peninsula jutting out amidst a pool of pungent, simmering tar. Instead of the hillside and the capped metal pipe, there was a gaping hole from which the tar was bubbling up, sputtering and spitting. Each bursting air pocket spewed nauseating fumes into the night. Kaitlin felt faint. She covered her mouth and nose.

"I *have* died," she said. "I've died and gone to hell." She was already on her knees, supported by Rindle, or she would have collapsed.

"You haven't died," he said. "But this is what I wanted to show you."

"But I didn't smell like that," she said, glancing around at the foul tar that almost surrounded them. "You said I stank. I would've smelled *that*."

"You couldn't. Not in the mundane world."

The mundane world. The normal world. She let his words wash over her without taking hold. Her mind grappled with her surroundings less successfully than did her senses, which were beginning to take stock. No other scent or taste penetrated the viscous miasma of the tar. The fumes coated the roof of her mouth, her tongue, throat, sinuses.

"Can we get out of here?" she asked.

Rindle helped her to her feet and led her away from the seething sludge. Beyond the pit, the night did not seem...right, normal. No buildings were visible. The incinerator compound was gone. A thick fog hung low to the ground, and what trees Kaitlin could see were branchless burned husks seeping black pus from their scarred trunks.

"Corruption. Decay," Rindle said. "This is the taint of the Wyrm. You smell it now?"

Did she smell it? It was all she could do to keep from vomiting. She felt a ball of thick black tar forming in the pit of her stomach.

The putrid corruption was hard to miss, but more slowly asserting itself into her awareness was not a presence but an absence, the ominous silence. Aside from the hissing and popping of the tar pit, the mist-shrouded night was silent. No sounds of night creatures, no trees rustling in the nonexistent breeze. Only the crackle and fizz of thick burbling decay.

"Okay. So you've shown me," she said, still not able to take it all in, not wanting to. "Can we go now?"

Rindle nodded. "Stay close. The paths in this place are not what you're accustomed to."

Kaitlin didn't understand, but she wanted to get away from there; demanding an explanation of what had happened and where they were would only make getting away take longer. So she followed Rindle closely. He had been restrained in dealing with her, but he too was obviously disturbed by their surroundings. He constantly scanned the area and peered into the mists, as if expecting something to charge out at any second. He moved not clumsily but stiffly, his every muscle tensed. His agitation undermined her own attempt to remain calm, but she fought the lurking panic; she resisted the urge to argue, to condemn him for bringing her here to this alien landscape.

As they walked, Kaitlin noticed a peculiar sensation: not of weightlessness, because there remained a definite up and down and this way and that, but she felt at times that her feet were landing on nothing. She could not feel the pressure of the earth beneath her boots. But the sensation was like catching sight of something in peripheral vision and turning, only to find nothing there. When she looked down, she saw her feet touching the ground. If she thought about it, she felt it as well. But when her thoughts started to wander—where the hell was this place? *what* was this place? how had they gotten here?— then the dislocation from physical reality crept back into the very fringes of her awareness—only to disappear again when she took notice.

Looking up from her feet, she saw that the scene around her had inexplicably changed: The trees that she and Rindle now passed were not charred, not shorn of branches and crowns. There were few enough of them—with the obscuring fog, never more than a handful ever seemed visible at once—but they were robust specimens, thick and old and healthy. The stink of the tar—Wyrm-taint, Rindle called it; the stench of corruption— was not as overpowering here, though the two travelers seemed to be picking out a course parallel to a shallow ditch in which the bubbling, creeping substance flowed along like black semi-coagulated blood.

"Are we following this?" Kaitlin asked.

"Yes."

"Why? I thought you wanted to get away from the stink."

"I have a bad feeling about this."

"And so you want to follow it?"

"We're almost...there." With his last word, the world around Kaitlin rippled like a pond broken by a stone. Rindle, after shimmering briefly, remained, though he seemed to have skipped a stride. The rest of the forest shifted as well. Kaitlin found herself amidst a different configuration of trees, and the ditch and its cargo of black ichor now emptied into a small stream. Where the two liquids met foul steam hissed and snaked into the air.

Rindle stood at the juncture, a deepening scowl apparent on his face. He scratched at the stubble on his chin. "Look," he said, pointing to a tree at the edge of the stream. The tree was healthy enough, but where its exposed roots dipped into the water, they were black and rotten, and to Kaitlin's amazement, she could see the water already drawn *within* the tree; she could see black sap circulating throughout the trunk and branches like contaminated blood; she could see the leaves growing brittle.

Leaves? "This is crazy," she said. "It's still winter. There shouldn't be leaves on this tree...and and and...and I can see inside it. I mean, it's not cut open or anything, but I can see inside it."

Rindle regarded her calmly. Too damn calmly, humoring her like one might a child. "The seasons are not so pronounced here. And I'm surprised you can see the corruption within the tree."

"What's that supposed to mean?"

"Just what I said. I thought for a time that you might be a creature of this world, a spirit of the Umbra, but I was foolish. You do seem to have a potent sight, though. Strange."

"You've got a lot of room to talk, Mr. Never-Killed-Anybody-That-Didn't-Deserve-It." She had known from the start that he was weird—even setting aside what she knew deep down: that he wasn't quite human—but the fact that he seemed to understand what was going on here...*that* proved her point once and for all. This was not the world outside her door; this forest was not the one surrounding her home—or at least not how she usually saw it. Even if she had gone totally and irrevocably insane, that didn't absolve Rindle from his derangement. And the more Kaitlin thought about it, the more she wished that she had, in fact, gone insane. That would mean that none of this was happening. The strange forest, the foul bubbling corruption, the mist that would not recede—none of it would be real.

But Kaitlin had seen strange things before. Impossible things. But even in her resolve to escape them, to ignore or deny, she had never been able to convince herself that she didn't see them. There were impossible, inexplicable things in the world. Why not an impossible, inexplicable world? She looked up to Rindle. His face was grim, and he seemed unaware of her, lost as he was in his own private thoughts.

Black Rindle stared at the stringy tendrils of corruption running through the stream. He had shown Kaitlin what he had brought her to see—he couldn't imagine her ever going back to that place to work—but he'd also found far more than he had expected. This stream was not a stranger to him. He'd not followed it this point for many a year, because Cloudkill had demanded members of the sept stay away from areas that humans frequented. But Black Rindle knew this spot. The incinerator, whatever was spawning the corruption, was not incredibly new. He tried to remember when exactly it had been built and this area had fallen off limits to the Garou. Three years ago? Four?

He had no doubt about what it was he saw before him. His indecision arose in deciding what to do about it. His stomach churned at the sight and the smell of the tainted stream. He wanted to strike out against the Wyrm. That was why he was put upon the world—if one gave credence to the old tales that EveSong told.

But thinking of EveSong and his stories roiled Black Rindle's insides almost as much as did the whiff of corruption. He could not fight this menace alone, he felt certain. But the Sept of the Wailing Glade, the only family he'd ever had or known, had rejected him, cast him out. How could he go to them now? Why should he? This was their problem. They'd made it clear enough that they wanted nothing to do with him ever again.

When he glanced at Kaitlin, however, he felt a need to protect her. Even if she didn't go back to the incinerator, with this type of menace lurking in the wilds, spreading, she would never be safe. He fidgeted where he stood, uncomfortable assuming that type of responsibility for her—but he felt it in his heart. He tried to see away around it: he didn't want to go back to the caern; he didn't want to face again those who so thoroughly despised him; he didn't want to feel EveSong's scorn, his own father's deep-seated animosity. But to save Kaitlin he had to save his sept. They had to be warned.

He looked at Kaitlin again, reminded himself of all the aggravation she caused him. Was she really worth all this?

Kaitlin didn't like this place. She didn't belong here, and she knew it. She felt it in her gut, in her bones. On top of that, Rindle kept looking at her funny. He would stand at stare at the stream, and then he would look over at her...strangely. Strangely even for him. Maybe it was her imagination. But she didn't think so.

"Come on," Rindle said at last.

Kaitlin was too confused by this place to argue. She tried to watch everything as she followed, but the landscape flowed in a way that defied her senses. She had the impression that miles fell away beneath each step. Each time she put her foot down, the world was new. The stream was beside her, and mist and trees, but the place her foot touched was not where she'd set out to put it; when she looked back, the scene she saw was not where she'd just been.

Rindle appeared unfazed. His attention was riveted on the stream and the streaks of corruption that spread through it like veins of liquid obsidian through marble. As he and she progressed, the veins grew less pronounced, less obvious, sometimes dipping below the surface of the water, in other appearing to disappear altogether only reappear shortly thereafter.

Before long, the surreal assault on Kaitlin's senses began to take its toll. Her vision blurred and she felt her eyes beginning to cross; only concerted effort kept the elusive wilderness backdrop in focus. Her eyes hurt, and the pain soon spread to her temples, her ears, the base of her skull.

A creature of this world, a spirit of the Umbra. That was what Black Rindle had said he'd thought she was. "I don't think so," Kaitlin mumbled. She could feel that she didn't belong here, that she could not long survive without snapping. Whatever the Umbra was, she didn't want any part of it. Her being here was wrong somehow. She felt similarly to the way she did when she saw one of the ephemeral specters in the city, or one of the phantasms lurking within a person walking down the street. She saw things that she shouldn't see, and seeing them was like opening a window into a forbidden world.

Now she had stepped full-blown into a forbidden world— maybe not the same world, because she didn't sense the same futility and longing that she did from the phantasms, but a world that wasn't meant for her, nonetheless.

She was loath to ask Rindle to rest. If anything, his pace was quickening, and as they covered more ground the disconnect among what Kaitlin saw and sensed and felt grew more intense. Had that step covered a mile, or two, or a hundred? Her muscles, taut with anxiety, began to burn. The pounding against her skull drowned out the burbling of the stream, which seemed practically free of the black veins now. As the pressure rose to the point that Kaitlin thought her head would surely explode, Rindle stopped.

She dropped to her knees and gasped for air like a drowning person, but Rindle seemed not to notice. He was intent upon a strange pile of rocks; it seemed to make a wall of sorts, with one end dipping into the stream itself.

He touched the stones and seemed puzzled. "Water Snake?" he said. "Water Snake, have you left us?"

Kaitlin didn't trust her perceptions at this point, but she had the distinct impression that Rindle was talking to the rocks. Disturbing as that was, she was relieved that the pounding in her head was receding. Now that they were stationary, the disorientation seemed gradually to be fading. Maybe in a few more minutes she would have been up to taking issue with the behavior of her companion, but they didn't have a few more minutes.

Kaitlin and Rindle were no longer alone. A huge snarling wolf-thing now stood just beyond the low stonewall, where a second before there had been only mist. Kaitlin's throat and stomach seized up with the terror she remembered from facing just such a creature before.

And then another appeared. From nowhere. It was simply there, standing upright, hackles raised, snarling and growling. Visions flashed through Kaitlin's mind of mangled bodies lying on the floor of the bar. Though death stared her in the face, she was too exhausted to run. She looked to Rindle—

—And he, too, was a huge, snarling man-wolf.

Chapter 19

Claudia Stands Firm was the first to step across from the mundane world. The Warder must have sensed Black Rindle's presence; whether she had expected to find him specifically seemed to make little difference. She growled and bared her fangs. She snarled a truncated ululation that summoned the others of the sept, and in a few seconds they joined her: Shreds Birch, Cynthia Slack Ear, EveSong, Barks-at-Shadows; only Night Terror and Cloudkill were absent. Growling and pawing at the ground, they spread in a wide semi-circle around Black Rindle and Kaitlin and gave indication of preparing to tear the two to shreds.

Black Rindle shifted to man-wolf as soon as he saw Stands Firm's fierce disposition. She wore Crinos and held her klaive before her. If she, harsh but levelheaded among the Garou, were ready for blood, Black Rindle knew he was in dire trouble. "There is Wyrm-taint spreading through the stream," he told them in the guttural barks of Garou-tongue. "It hasn't yet come this far—"

"Haven't you already done enough?" EveSong snarled. "*You* are the corruption of this sept. Gaia spites us because of your—"

"I did not taint the stream," Black Rindle cut him off. "That was the Wyrm's doing. But I can show you—"

"He stinks of the Wyrm!" Shreds Birch growled. "He comes here stinking of corruption the night after Frederich is killed!"

Black Rindle's ears twitched; he stared, stupefied, at the others. "Night Terror killed? But how...?"

"Poison," Slack Ear growled.

"Poisoned cattle at the Davidson farm," EveSong said through clenched fangs. "Poison and then attack by humans immune to the Delirium." He glared menacingly at Kaitlin.

"And now he brings one *here!*" said Shreds Birch. She was Lupus and low to the ground; she edged closer to Kaitlin, growling.

Kaitlin was frozen and wide-eyed with terror, but it was true that she was not seized by the insanity of the Delirium, as Black Rindle had seen before. Whatever the cause, it was not in her favor with the mood of the sept. "This girl had nothing to do with Night Terror's death," Black Rindle said. "She helped me find the source of the Wyrm-taint. It spreads this way. We must protect the stream before the caern itself is fouled. Look! Already Water Snake does not respond to our presence. We must—"

"Water Snake is offended by *your* presence!" EveSong spat. "They lured us with poisoned cattle at the farm. The girl lures you to the Wyrm. You were only a step away from corruption from the start! You rotted Galia from within, and now you look to taint the caern!"

Black Rindle stepped forward threateningly. Almost imperceptibly, the semi-circle of Garou edged back, but Black Rindle noticed. He knew also the thin line he toed: between provoking an attack through belligerence or inviting one through weakness. His chances, and Kaitlin's, were not good if violence erupted. And with Garou, violence was never far below the surface. He was only trying to warn them. They didn't have to take him back. All they had to do was listen. But Night Terror had fallen, and the Garou were in no mood for conversation.

"Claudia," Black Rindle appealed to the more reasonable Warder. "You know I had nothing to do with Frederich's death. You know I've never submitted—never come *close* to submitting—to Wyrm-taint. Tell them."

All eyes turned to Stands Firm. She did not relish the attention. She regarded Black Rindle warily, then said: "The girl—how is it that she stands here, watching, listening? Is she human—or Wyrm-creature?"

Kaitlin had understood none of the growled and barked conversation, but now when all eyes turned to her, she shrank back. Black Rindle hoped she wouldn't break and run. He wouldn't be able to protect her; they would bring her down in seconds if she did. He edged closer to her, positioning himself between her and as many of the Garou as he could. He wanted them to understand that he vouched for her, that she was here under his protection—whatever little good that might do.

"I do not know how it is that she can see us and not flee," he admitted. "Perhaps Kinfolk blood runs in her veins, and she doesn't know...or Gaia has simply smiled upon her." He was fishing for anything that sounded plausible. His audience was not receptive. "But she is not of the Wyrm. I would know."

"She stinks of it," Shreds Birch snarled.

"I told you, she helped me find the source of the danger to the stream," Black Rindle said. "But the stream is only the beginning. Already the corruption creeps through the land. It seeps into the trees. Follow me and I'll show you. Don't take my word for it. Let me *show you*."

"Wyrm-spawn!" EveSong howled.

"Damn you!" Black Rindle yelled back. "Listen to me or you're dooming all the land! It's dying. The spirits have left. We haven't served them. They are angry. Balthazar saw it when he took my mother, and he was right. We must—"

"Wyrm-spawn!"

"Wyrm-spawn!" Shreds Birch took up the cry. "Wyrm-spawn!"

And Slack Ear as well. "Wyrm-spawn!"

Stands Firm seemed hesitant to condemn him, but neither did she offer support. Barks-at-Shadows, who had mostly watched and who appeared the least belligerent, looked unsettled by the flaring hostility, but even he was growing more agitated, snarling and showing his teeth.

"Listen to me!" Black Rindle shouted, knowing it was useless but hoping somehow to break the rising pitch of the howl. He reached behind him, touched Kaitlin's arm; he couldn't spare a glance, but he wanted to make sure she was near. Even as he yowled and snarled at EveSong to be quiet, Black Rindle kept his eyes on Stands Firm. If the Warder joined her voice to the rolling condemnation, then all was lost. At the same time, he had to fight down his own rage. It was a struggle not to pounce on EveSong, not to rip open his throat and make the others listen. But they would not listen.

"Enough!" called a powerful voice.

And the howl fell silent. They all turned as one and beheld Evert Cloudkill. He stood before them, a magnificent Crinos, blood dripping from his claws. His own blood. For along the length of his chest were deep, raking gashes. He held his claws before him. The semi-circle opened for him to step through and face Black Rindle.

Black Rindle saw the bloody gashes and retreated several steps. The wounds were his fault. They *must* be. Just as every indignity and injury that Cloudkill had suffered since the day Black Rindle was born was Black Rindle's fault. All thought of combating the Wyrm or of making the others believe him fled at the sight of his father.

"Who is this?" Cloudkill said, but it was not Kaitlin of whom he spoke. In fact, he seemed oblivious to her presence. His eyes bore into Black Rindle alone. The other Garou might as well not have been there. "Who is this that is dead to me? Who would come to torment me after my love has passed from the world? Were you in league with that Strider? Came to watch over her, he said. And then he steals away her body in the dark of night. Who is this that comes the day that my septmate is slain and brings a human—a human who might well be a creature of the Wyrm? He brings her to the caern. Would you let her violate our places of power? Do you hate me so much that you would see all that I have built destroyed?"

Black Rindle stood mute, unable to refute the arguments of Cloudkill, who seemed animated purely by hatred. Thus had it always been: impudent child, metis, nipping at the heels until he was slapped down. How could he contest the word of his father, of the sept alpha, builder of the caern? Black Rindle shrank back. He felt his hunch weighing him down; he felt the half-ring of Garou closing in again, murderous rage flashing in their eyes. But there was more than his own failings at stake, and Black Rindle drew strength from the urgency of his news, and of his newfound purpose.

"There is corruption spreading this way," he said, trying with his own calm to dampen the bloodlust that filled the air. "It follows the route of the stream—from the incinerator west of the town."

Cloudkill sighed. He had no hunch, but the weight of profound sorrow stooped his shoulders. "This caern is the light that keeps corruption at bay."

"But just go look—!"

Cloudkill raised a bloody claw and silenced his denounced progeny. "Owl and Water Snake both guard and protect us. We have nothing to fear." He drew himself up straight, taller than the cowed Black Rindle.

"But the corruption must be too strong," Black Rindle insisted. "It's spreading. Owl and Water Snake—"

"Enough!" Cloudkill said for a second time. "I will hear no more."

"You haven't heard anything I've said yet!" Black Rindle dared. "Ever!"

Cloudkill turned his back on Black Rindle and spoke instead to the assembled Garou of the sept. "This one is cast out. He has returned against my command and endangered the caern by consorting with a Wyrm-tainted human. No punishment is too severe. See that he never harms us again."

A victorious, vicious howl of pure bloodlust went up amongst the Garou, but before the first calls for Black Rindle's hide had escaped their mouths, he had snatched up Kaitlin and fled into the Umbral forest. The hunters were not long behind their prey.

Chapter 20

Rindle almost whip-lashed Kaitlin when he yanked her off her feet, and she bit her lip almost clean through. But she was grateful.

For the few minutes she'd been standing among those beasts, she'd been sure that she was about to die. That could still happen. Would happen, unless Rindle—one of the beasts—could escape the others. Despite his hunch and awkward gait, he raced through the blurring forest with her clutched to his chest like a baby. If before Kaitlin's head had hurt because of the discontinuous landscape, now, hurled along at the speed of Rindle's power and desperation, she retreated into her personal place of solitude. She could not comprehend the flashing scenery; she tried to let the mist cloud everything from her mind. There were only the rough jostling and Rindle's labored breathing. She closed her eyes and imagined herself beneath her quilt, all the world closed out.

But she could not escape the howling. The hungry, maniacal baying of beasts intent on murder. What had passed among them she had no way of knowing. For a few moments, they had studied her intently. Their palpable hostility suggested claws and teeth to come. She folded her arms and clutched them across her belly. Maybe they would kill her quickly. She didn't want her insides spread over the floor of this forest that didn't even feel like a real place to her. Would anyone ever find her?

Would her family find out what had happened? Would they care?

The howling crept closer. A trick of the woods, she thought. She hoped. As quickly as Rindle was moving, could the others be faster?

She tasted her tears, and the blood from her lip. She tried to keep her whimperings soft, so as not to distract Rindle. A missed step could be the end of them. The others were not falling behind or giving up.

When next she looked up, Kaitlin saw what only by instinct she knew to be her house. Not the house as she'd ever seen it. The road was gone, and the yard was a rolling expanse of periwinkle in bloom, a violet carpet that would have been beautiful were it not for the frantic retreat and the blood-curling howls now hot on their heels. The house itself was no house at all—no walls, no roof, but merely the hardwood floors and the staircase seemingly supporting the upper level. On the suspended second story floor was Kaitlin's bed, covered by her quilt. No other furniture, no other signs of habitation.

As Kaitlin tried to absorb what she was seeing, Rindle seemed to stutter step, and for a moment they, like the upper floor, were suspended in space. In time, too, it seemed. Rindle's breath, growing ragged with exertion, paused...and took back up mid pant. During that instant, Kaitlin felt the shock of cold water again, as if she'd jumped back into the lake—or out of it. For the world changed as she sucked in her breath, changed back to what it should have been all along. To the forest of densely packed trees and underbrush. To a sky not obscured by enveloping mist, to a house that had walls and roof and windows and doors. Kaitlin knew the relief of waking from a nightmare.

But then she heard the howling still behind her. She felt every jarring step as Rindle, still a monstrous beast, sprinted across her yard. The nightmare was not left behind in that other world. It was here. It was following her. And it wanted her blood.

Rindle hardly slowed when he ripped open the front door. A window in the next room shattered, a blurred figure hurtling through the glass. Claws dug into the hardwood as the desperate race drew to a close. Kaitlin couldn't breathe. They'd made it back home—but that wasn't good enough. The beasts of rage had made it too.

Through the kitchen. Rindle whipped open the door to the basement, took all the stairs in two steps. He dumped Kaitlin roughly into a corner and then turned to face the claws that already were at his throat.

All the snarling and howling to this point were nothing compared to the uproar that commenced but feet away from Kaitlin. She pressed herself back farther into the corner—the same corner where once she'd hidden from Rindle. Water splattered on her face—not water; she wiped her face and smelled blood, smearing it with her hand.

In the darkness, all she could make out were the flurry of motion and the flashing of teeth and claws. The snarling now was underscored by the snap of jaws clamping shut—on air with fang rattling against fang, or on flesh and bone accompanied by yowls of pain and anger. Here another dark shape charged in, there a body flung itself, or was flung, across the room. Was that a flash of silver? Kaitlin tried to count how many combatants assailed Rindle: more than one definitely, but how many more? Two, three, all that had been assembled by the stream?

Unless Rindle could overcome them all, he and she were doomed. The howling beasts were out for blood. There would be no quarter given.

And then suddenly it all stopped. The murderous yowling and barking dropped away to throaty growls. The bodies weren't throwing themselves at each other, or biting and clawing. A half-crouched figure backed into Kaitlin. Deciding that if it was one of the others, she'd likely be dead already, she reached up, felt the rough curve of Rindle's hump, and was sure it was him. She felt blood on his fur, also. Her hand came away with clumps of bloody matted fur sticking to it.

"Are you all right?" she asked him—almost choking on the meaninglessness of the words as she spoke them. All right? How could he, how could anything, be all right? All right could only be measured in terms of: not dead yet.

Rindle grunted—whatever that meant. But he was still standing.

As her eyes started to adjust to the darkness, Kaitlin saw other pairs of eyes, red and glaring, far from abandoning bloodshed. They formed an arc, much like the beasts had at the stonewall. Rindle reached back and grabbed her shoulder.

"You…get out?" he asked, though she barely recognized his voice, deep, guttural, labored. She tried to imagine human speech emerging from those deadly jaws and decided she was glad there was no light. But the question was well taken.

Could she get out? Not past the monsters and up the stairs. But this was an unfinished basement. Aside from the two tiny windows, which she couldn't reach, wasn't there a crawl space somewhere? Could she make her way unobserved to the front of the house and out beneath the porch. Maybe. But in the dark, without running into one of those beasts first? And if she did, then what? Run away into the woods so these things could track her down when they were done with him?

"No," she said, pulling on his arm. "No." She would not leave him.

He grunted again, and almost instantly launched himself at the other monsters. The gruesome noises of lethal combat resumed, more fiercely even than before, if that was possible. Kaitlin couldn't bear to watch. Through the darkness, she stared helplessly at her own hands, at the bloody fur that clung to them. She waited in vain for some sense of revulsion at the sight, but fear had bludgeoned her to numbness; she could not be more frightened: for Rindle, but she could not help him; for her own skin, if all of this incomprehensible night was real; for her mind, if it was not. How she prayed for insanity as the snarling and snapping of jaws grew closer.

One of the raging beasts roared in agony. Was it Rindle? She couldn't tell the sounds apart; she couldn't see anything but swirling, violently churning bodies—

But then suddenly she *could* see them: a confused melee of frothing, bloody beasts, werewolves of myth and legend. Rindle was in their midst, his coat thick with blood, one side of his face laid open. One of the others limped away from the heap, his arm hanging useless at his side, torn open to the bone. Three or four others hammered and bit and clawed at Rindle. Kaitlin couldn't tell exactly how many there were, so fast and ferocious was the action. But they all lashed out at Rindle. Their claws were wet with his blood. They would kill him. Soon. Every inch of his body shone like a red-black oil slick.

No. There was another. Fighting not against Rindle but with him, if Kaitlin could believe her eyes. She hadn't noticed him at first amidst the jumble of bodies, all strength and fur and rage. Even now she lost track of this one, who she didn't recall seeing at the stonewall. But it was so hard to know. In the writhing mass, it was difficult to know who an arm or a leg belonged to. They moved too quickly. The whole pack was constantly shifting for position, lunging, swiping, dodging. To Kaitlin's horror, at least one arm was lying on the floor—connected to no one. She looked desperately for Rindle amidst the fray. There. One arm, two arms. Though he could barely see for the blood streaming over his face.

She caught sight of the newcomer again. She saw now that he was larger than the rest. She distrusted her first impression, but he *was* fighting with Rindle. A backhanded swipe of a powerful hand cracked the skull of another attacker. He staggered a step from the fight and collapsed. The odds evened slightly.

As they fought on, Kaitlin realized why the newcomer was so difficult to follow among the others. While their coats were mono-hued or mottled, his was a mosaic of interspersed patches, each a different color of fur. Now that she knew what she was watching, Kaitlin also realized that among all the combatants, he was the only one not covered in blood. Furthermore, the sudden light that had revealed to her the deadly struggle—it seemed to emanate from this great wolf.

The fight continued to thin out, and as the more severely mauled creatures fell away, the great size of the Patchwork Wolf became readily apparent: He was easily twice Kaitlin's height, and unable to stand fully erect in the basement. The confining space, however, seemed no disadvantage to him. He knocked aside every attack directed at him, and some aimed at Rindle. As the tight clump of bodies broke apart, the three remaining attackers eyed him warily. None of the creatures, save he, was unscathed.

A brief lull ensued, the savages on both sides taking measure of one another, divining the condition of opponents, searching for a weakness or injury that would allow a killing blow. The respite was brief, but a few seconds, and then by design or by instinct the attackers pounced, three at once.

A pair of them struck at Rindle. He countered the one, but the second sank his fangs into Rindle's side. He snarled in pain as with his own fangs he clamped down on the forearm of the first assailant. The second attacker, within Rindle's guard, struck with lightning-fast raking claws—

—Until he was pulled away by the great Patchwork Wolf, who held his opponent in one mighty hand, suspended by the neck a foot above the floor. The creature dragged from Rindle could not resist the strength of the giant man-wolf. The

Patchwork Wolf slammed the two creatures together and then cast them effortlessly against the far wall.

The only remaining struggle was between Rindle and the beast whose arm was firmly between his fangs. Rindle bit down and shook with all his might, his victim yowling in pain but unable to escape. A hard cuff from the Patchwork Wolf this time sent Rindle sprawling, and the other man-wolf staggered back, favoring his ruined arm.

For a moment, silence reigned. Aside from the luminescent Patchwork Wolf, the beasts all lay stunned and battered. Kaitlin watched in awe, afraid that the victor would continue his attack against Rindle—against her. She didn't understand why the newcomer had helped Rindle and then turned on him so. Rindle, shaking his head and coming to his senses, seemed to wonder the same thing.

And then the Patchwork Wolf spoke: "This—must—stop." The words came forth rumbling from deep within his chest and rattled the foundation of the house. The ferocity he'd shown in battle was far from gone; he looked and sounded as if he were struggling not to lash out, to continue the fight—but for which side? His glare swept the room, encompassing each werewolf in turn. "Garou—does—not—kill—Garou."

Watching him, Kaitlin knew what Rindle had meant when he'd mentioned a creature of spirit. This creature was not like the specters and demons that she had seen in the city. The Patchwork Wolf, though horrendous to behold, was a magnificent beast. He shimmered in her sight; luminescent, otherworldly, he was a creature of spirit. And looking on the others, no longer blinded by fear and denial, Kaitlin could see a spark of him within each of them, a fragment of spirit which animated their passions.

The Patchwork Wolf reached out and lifted Rindle to his feet. "This one is not the enemy," the spirit wolf said. He placed a hand on Rindle's chest and wiped the blood from the eyes of the smaller man-wolf. "And they are not your enemy," he said. "You must forgive the past and look to the future. I impart to you that gift."

Rindle staggered beneath the weight of that massive hand, but he did not fall. Tears came to Kaitlin's eyes; she was unsure why. The cumulative tension of being lost, fearing for her life, witnessing salvation. She slumped to the floor, the weight of hope and of the future too much for her to bear.

But the Patchwork Wolf came to her side, lifted her to her feet, supported her when her legs nearly failed her. "Neither is this one the enemy," he said. "You must look to yourselves. The spirits do not forsake their children without reason. Be wise. Be strong."

And he was gone. The light with him. But as the other werewolves straggled away in confused silence, a sheath of light shone down the stairs from above. Kaitlin ran to Rindle. She embraced him, not dissuaded by the blood that covered him. She tried to support him as his knees buckled, but he was too heavy for her. They crumpled to the floor together, and when they came to rest, it was a man, bleeding and exhausted and delirious, whose head she cradled in her lap.

Chapter 21

Black Rindle flinched and drew in a sharp breath.

"I'm sorry, I'm sorry," Kaitlin said, dabbing with a wet cloth at the edges of the gouge in his shoulder. "I'm trying to be easy, but it's going to hurt some. I don't think there's any getting around that. Here." She raised a glass of water to his lips. Her hands were still trembling slightly from what she and Black Rindle had just been through.

"I'd rather have something stronger," he said, sipping at the water.

"Yeah, well, that's not going to happen. *Somebody* drank all the beer, and I'm sure as hell not going to run across the street and get something from your friend at the Tap House."

Black Rindle was quickly coming to believe that sobriety was overrated. He was lying on Kaitlin's bed while she tended the painful, slow-healing wounds he'd suffered at the claws and teeth of his former septmates. Not only would he have been hurting a lot less now if he were drunk, if he'd been drunk the past few days he'd never have gotten into this mess. If he'd been drunk, he wouldn't have bothered poking around at the incinerator; if he'd been drunk, he wouldn't have followed the strangled stream back to the caern; he wouldn't have gotten his ass kicked. Again.

Black Rindle sighed, and even that hurt. "I try to follow his advice, and this is what I get," he said, disgruntled.

"What are you talking about? Whose advice?"

"Meneghwo."

"What-ghwo?"

"The one who saved me," Black Rindle said. "Saved us."

Despite the obvious reminder of the ragged gashes all over Black Rindle, mentioning the fight seemed to undo Kaitlin's relative calm. Her hands began to quiver more violently, so much that she spilled water from the glass Black Rindle had handed back to her.

"The Quilt Wolf," she said.

"Quilt?" Black Rindle watched her very closely. Had she taken a blow to the head that he wasn't aware of?

"Quilt. Patchwork. It all fits," Kaitlin said. "All those different patches of fur." She tapped the quilt, which Black Rindle was lying on, bleeding on. "It's like this. Little pieces from...from God knows where, but each someplace different. And then you put them all together, and you have this whole, new..."

"Ugly, mongrel..." Black Rindle supplied the adjectives.

"*Beautiful* thing," Kaitlin insisted, scowling at him. "You know, you sure are stuck on physical appearance...for somebody who has a big hump on your back."

Black Rindle jerked away from her, refused to let her tend his wounds. "I don't need your help," he snapped.

Kaitlin drew her hands back, raised them as if in surrender. "I know, I know. You don't need anybody's help. I've been there." After a few minutes, she began dabbing at his shoulder again, and Black Rindle grudgingly let her. "I was just thinking about him this morning, that's all," she said, "and he reminded me of my quilt. What'd you say his name was?"

"Meneghwo."

"Really." She paused from washing him. "Do any of your friends *not* have weird names? Although I have to say," she continued before he could answer, "I'm glad your name is Black Rindle and not Blackie Hunchback. Blackie doesn't fit you."

"And why's that?"

"I don't know. Blackie sounds like somebody who might be fun once in a while. You, on the other hand, are always in a bad mood. You are the most surly person I have ever met. *And* the only time you take me out, you try to get me killed."

Black Rindle glared at her with equal parts aggravation and amazement. Was this her way of coping with trauma: by antagonizing him? "You know," he said, "you're not exactly a bundle of joy."

Kaitlin wiped his wound a bit less gingerly and he winced. "You are such a baby," she said. "Sure, you go around ripping people's arms off, but a little soap and water and you squeal like a..."

"Like a girl?"

"Pig. You squeal like a pig."

Black Rindle decided to let the comment slide. He suspected that agitating Kaitlin further would only prod her overzealous cleansing of his injuries. Still, not since he was a young pup and Galia had taken care of him had anyone wanted to tend to him. He closed his eyes, tried to ignore the pain and rest secure in the knowledge that this woman wanted to help him. She wasn't doing this out of fear. Out of obligation? Perhaps. But did it matter? When was the last time anyone had felt any obligation toward him. A few sarcastic indignities was small enough a price to pay for the comfort, besides which, he was not blind to the fact that last night had been traumatic for Kaitlin. Far more traumatic for her than it had been for him. He, too, had faced near-certain death, but at the hands of individuals he had always known—of a race of creature that he had always known existed. How terrifyingly surreal it all must have seemed to Kaitlin. If she was a bit agitated, she was due. She had not asked him to drag her through the Umbra and plop her in the middle of a seething, murderous sept of Garou.

"Why were they so angry?" she asked at last, pensively, as if reading the context of his silence. "Why did they want to kill us? Did *we* deserve it."

Black Rindle kept his eyes close; he didn't want to see on her face the hurt he heard in her voice. She seemed to take it personally that they'd wanted to kill her. Humans were sheltered in that way. "*They* would have said that we deserved it."

"Why?"

"Me, because my very existence is a sign of corruption. You...because you were there, and they were angry. And because you see us."

"That makes me what—dangerous?"

"Could. Most humans, if they do see us, they flip out, lose it, go insane. At least for a while. And then later they don't really remember. They remember *something*, but not much. They feel scared and sick, and maybe some weird rumors spread around. But you..."

"I saw you in front of the bar last week," Kaitlin said.

"I know."

Silence.

"You did have a body over your shoulder, didn't you?"

"I did," Black Rindle said. "And, yes, he deserved it. He and his friend would've killed me and EveSong—Murphy, that is— for twenty bucks. For no reason, really. Just for the thrill."

"And is it a thrill for you?"

Black Rindle opened his eyes. He would take only so much—but he could not completely disavow her question. He never felt so alive, so attuned to Gaia and all of creation, as in those few seconds of the hunt just before the kill. "It's never *just* that." He closed his eyes again.

Kaitlin evidently recognized his line in the sand. She returned her attention to cleaning the bloody gashes. Her ministrations were again gentle and, a few minutes later when she spoke again, her next question was not so sharp. "What did you mean about your existence being a sign of corruption?"

Black Rindle sighed. "It is forbidden for our kind to mate one with another. We must find partners beyond our people, among humans or wolves."

"You actually breed with wolves?"

"Some of us are much closer to wolves than to human."

"But what does the taboo have to do with—"

"I am what happens when two of our people mate: an accursed cub, an affront to Gaia." Black Rindle opened his eyes and sat up; she was to give him no peace.

"That's why they hate you?" Kaitlin asked incredulously. The answer angered her. "It's hardly *your* fault that—"

"No matter whose fault," he said, "the burden is mine to bear."

But she was having none of that. "It's just…it's…it's *wrong*. It's as wrong as the people who hate me because I'm black. It's ignorant. It's small-minded."

"Among humans, is it not a crime for brother to mate with sister?"

"Well…yes, but that's not the same—"

"Not exactly the same, no," he said. "But I am deformed. I am not human, not wolf, but among the Garou I am despised."

"Garou," Kaitlin repeated. "You keep using that name. Meneghwo used it too. Your people, your race are the Garou."

Black Rindle struggled to sit up more, to look directly into her eyes. "Some of this you see for yourself. Some of it you learn from me. None of it can you pass on to other humans. Our name is not for humans of this age of the world. I do not understand why it is that you are able to see what you do—but it is one reason the others wanted to kill us. They see you as a threat, and others of my kind will also."

"But why?" she wanted to know. "You think *I'm* a threat to *you*? When you change, when you become a werewolf, you are huge and powerful and ferocious. How in the world could humans harm you?"

"You could say the same about bear or lions or sharks. How do humans harm them? They hunt them. They destroy their habitat. Humans are part of the problem. They are the despoilers of Gaia."

"Like the Wyrm-taint," she said. "Corruption."

"In a way, but not so simple," Black Rindle corrected her. "Human devastation encourages the spread of Wyrm-taint, and Wyrm-taint feeds into human devastation, but which is the cause and which is the effect—the answer to that question is buried in time. There is also the Weaver to consider, but she does not have such a great hold here in the forested lands. But go to one of the scabs, one of your cities…"

Kaitlin held up her hands. "Okay, okay, okay. I think that's about all I can take at one time, all right? And yeah, I'll remember, my lips are sealed. And you know what else? Your friends are some ignorant, perverse bastards."

Black Rindle started to respond, started to lash out at her harping, but he found himself speechless in the face of her criticism of his septmates. Why should he defend those who had cast him out? He had often thought the same thing that Kaitlin had said, and much worse, but he'd always felt guilty for his resentment. He was the accursed of Gaia. Of course the others despised him. Never—not *once*—had another person joined him in maligning the other Garou. Not since he was a cub and Galia had stood up for him had anyone taken his side, and even she, cowed by Cloudkill's rantings, had fallen silent when Black Rindle grew older.

Now here was Kaitlin. He had treated her rudely and thoughtlessly placed her in danger. Yet it was the other Garou she denounced. She was standing up for *him*. Black Rindle felt the familiar, habitual twinge of guilt—but it was gratitude that robbed him of words.

"So what's next?" Kaitlin asked "Where do we...where do you go from here?"

"They made it pretty clear that I'm not wanted here. You heard what EveSong and Cloudkill said."

"Actually, I never got past *grrr*, and...well, you know."

"Oh. Right."

"But, yeah, I guess their meaning was clear enough. What about what Meneghwo said, though?"

"He said to look to the future. That doesn't mean the future has to be here," Black Rindle pointed out. "It will be easier for everyone if I go. That's what they want."

"And what about the black tar stuff, the stream, the Wyrm-taint?" Kaitlin asked. "Did you warn them about that? Do they know?"

"I warned them. They wouldn't listen."

"So it will keep spreading? What does that mean? What happens?"

"If no one combats it, then in time the land will die."

"The land will die?" The hard edge was creeping back into Kaitlin's voice. "What does that mean? The land will die."

Black Rindle shrugged. He wasn't inclined to elaborate. He wouldn't be around when it happened, so he wasn't going to think about it.

Kaitlin was growing increasingly frustrated with his refusal to answer her. "And you can walk away and let that happen—whatever exactly *that* is?"

She was like EveSong in a way, Black Rindle decided. She just couldn't stand to leave well enough alone. She always had to say one more thing, always had to ask one more question. He was tempted to get up and walk away, no matter how much he hurt, no matter she'd taken his side against his tormentors. But what the hell difference did that really make? They'd tried to kill her. He had tried to save her. *Of course* she'd taken his side. The worst part, though, was that she was right. Damnably, infuriatingly right. He couldn't simply turn his back on the threat of Wyrm-taint. Or maybe he could, but he *shouldn't*. He could still smell the wrongness of the insidious poison spreading through the land, corrupting the spirit of the water, the trees. How many years until the Umbral blight became manifest in the mundane world as well? Five, three, one? Would the trees fail to bud this spring? Would the forest die and the Garou's home become a wasteland? But even if he could make a difference, what was there to stay for? The shrine to Water Snake was now a pile of rocks, nothing more. Where was the wisdom of Owl? Menegwho confirmed that the spirits had turned their backs on the Wailing Glade. Shouldn't Black Rindle take that as a sign to do the same? And yet here was Kaitlin telling him that he should stay and fight. He saw another way.

"I can walk away," he said. "And you can come with me."

Kaitlin grew quiet, pensive. She looked away, as if Black Rindle had said something she'd thought but had been afraid to give voice. Finally, she shook her head, rejected him like so many others had. "I've already run away," she said. "I'm just starting to get back into the world. My world. I can't give up again."

Black Rindle nodded. It had taken him years to reach this point—years of scorn and abuse heaped upon him. His people had forsaken him; his own father had forsaken him. Why should this small, fragile human be any different? "I'm tired," he said, and then closed his eyes until he heard her footsteps retreating away from him down the hall.

Chapter 22

B lack Rindle recognized the dreamworld this time. He opened his eyes and sat upright on Kaitlin's bed. Her quilt was speckled with his blood, which had seeped from his many wounds. He wasn't sure what led him to believe he inhabited a dream: perhaps the way that vision seemed little more than a trick of the light, shimmering, ready to change the instant he looked away. What did it mean, he wondered, that he, in this dream, was whole of body, uninjured, yet his blood marked the quilt? The dreamworld, like the Umbra, was full of meaning for those who knew how to read the signs. But Black Rindle was no crescent moon. He was Ahroun, warrior born. To him, the dreamworld and the Umbra, as well as the mundane world at times, seemed capricious and cruel, whimsical and unpredictable.

He looked to the doorway of the bedroom, and there was Meneghwo, the great stitched-together wolf sitting upon his haunches.

"I thought you might be here," Black Rindle said. He tried to keep the bitterness from his voice. Meneghwo had saved his life, after all—his life and Kaitlin's as well. But what good had it done?

Meneghwo did not respond. He merely stared back through his mismatched eyes, one brown, one green.

"What?" Black Rindle asked, suspicious. "What do you want?" No answer. The silence irritated Black Rindle. So did the wolf's intent stare, slightly sorrowful, disappointed. *"What?"* Still the wolf did not respond. Black Rindle bristled. "I tried what you said. *Look to the future,*" he said scornfully. "I tried to warn them. I wanted to forge my own future. Look what it got me."

Black Rindle started to point at the bloodstains on the quilt, but the quilt was no longer a patchwork of fabric but of mismatched squares of fur, like Meneghwo. Except the hide-quilt was now covered in blood, not the mere speckles and splotches from Black Rindle's wounds. He drew back his blood-drenched hands.

"Why can't you leave me in peace?" he growled at the spirit wolf. "I know you said more than look to the future. 'Forgive the past.' Well, the best I can do is *forget* the past, so I'm moving on. I'm not turning my back on the Wyrm-threat, so don't look at me like that. I warned them. If they don't have the sense to listen…" Black Rindle flung aside the bloody pelt that had been the quilt. With every moment he grew more incensed at the Patchwork Wolf's silent accusation.

Black Rindle grew increasingly angry, too, because he had no idea what the future held. If he was moving on, he was moving on into a world of uncertainty. For the first time he faced and really understood the prospect of leaving this place, leaving his sept and all he had known, however unpleasant. Leaving Kaitlin.

That last shouldn't have mattered. She was just a human, more or less. But she had helped him when no other would. She had stood up for him. He had assumed somehow that she would leave this place with him, and not until she refused had he recognized how much he *wanted* her to leave with him. That admission to himself on top of everything else—that he wanted her to stay with him, that he valued her companionship—made him angry as well.

"I'm not running away!" he growled at Meneghwo, who cocked his head but offered word of neither rebuke or comfort. "I'm not running away!" Black Rindle said again, as he shifted to rage-form. He'd had enough of Meneghwo's silence. Black Rindle leapt from the bed, and when his feet touched the floor, it gave way beneath him.

Not as floor should—with a great crash and splintering of hardwood, plunging him down to the room below. This floor was the stuff of dreams, and gave way as an ocean, in an instant accepting Black Rindle into its midst.

He plunged far beneath the surface, and as shock receded and he tried to wrap his mind around the perfidious whims of the dreamworld, he found himself choking. Not on water. He gasped in pure corruption, boiling viscous tar that seared the inside of his mouth and throat. His lungs filled and burned. Coughing and spitting did no good. There was no air. Black Rindle thrashed and kicked, but he was lost in a sea of rot and decay, black as the bubbling pits he and Kaitlin had seen, black as his own name. He lashed out in terror and in fury. The *wrongness* of the corruption enraged him, even as it choked the breath from his body. He could find no other scent than its stench, no other sight than total darkness.

And then suddenly he broke the surface. He was sprawled on all fours, knee- and elbow-deep in putrid grey sludge. Spasms wracked his body, coughing, retching. The churning chaos of corruption receded, and there was only still, stagnant water. The taste and sting of Wyrm-taint clung in his mouth. His stomach and throat continued to spasm, trying to expunge the last of the foul substance.

Black Rindle climbed to his feet—tried to, at least, but banged his head and sank again to his knees. The walls of a subterranean tunnel, rough unhewn stone, surrounded him, hemmed him in. Where, he wondered, was the deep ocean of corruption that had overwhelmed him? This water carried the stink but was too shallow....

Something bright caught his attention, a flash of light amidst the murky water. Black Rindle thrust his hand beneath the surface and felt around frantically—*there*. He gripped a handle worn smooth by use and pulled from the water a silver blade, a Garou klaive. As he thought to wonder how it had come to be in that desolate, Gaia-forsaken place, he discovered that the blade was not all that hid beneath the surface of the rank water.

A ripple in the otherwise motionless stream caught his attention, and was followed by the sensation of something brushing against his knee. Black Rindle crawled backward. He poked the tip of the klaive into the water as if this liquid, like the black ocean before, might try to annihilate him, but the water, though foul, was passive, inert. Black Rindle poked deeper. He tried to peer into the depths—

—The tentacle that shot lightning-quick from the water struck at his face. Black Rindle lurched backward. He caught the tentacle in his right hand, slashed at it with the klaive in his left. The silver blade sliced through the tenebrous form, which, severed, splashed into the water.

Black Rindle met the second attack that followed almost immediately, and the third, and the fourth. Severed tips of tentacles flew into the darkness as if spit out by a fan. But another tentacle slithered beneath the water, ensnared his foot, and climbed, coiling, to his knee. More reached down from the ceiling, while the water fairly churned with rubbery appendages all intent on taking hold of the Garou. With claws and klaive, Black Rindle struck many of them down, but he had no room to maneuver, and tentacles loomed from practically every direction. They wrapped around his arms, curtailing his ability to fight; they pinned the klaive against a wall, though he still ripped apart a dozen tentacles through brute force; they snaked around his neck, constricting until spots danced before his eyes.

Before he knew it, they pulled Black Rindle from his feet. They dragged him, still struggling and thrashing, through the dank fetid water, along the length of the tunnel. At some point the klaive fell from his hand, though he could no longer free himself enough to swing it. He felt the strength draining from his body, and had almost resigned himself to his fate—until he saw where the tendrils were dragging him.

Seeing it came last. First he felt the stone and earthen tunnel open into a much larger chamber. Then he smelled the wet, musty stink of corruption, even stronger than it had been. He heard the ominous sound of bone scraping against bone—these were not true bones, though, but teeth. Teeth longer than his arm, like stalactites and stalagmites drawing together and apart, ready to rend whatever body the foul tentacles could drag within reach. That is what he saw. Black Rindle began to struggle anew, but the tendrils dragged him closer and closer.

And then suddenly he was free. He had shredded Kaitlin's quilt, as well as the mattress and the bedposts. Mangled fragments of pillow lay scattered around the room. Daylight shone beyond the windows—afternoon here in the mundane world.

Black Rindle looked to the doorway but saw no sign of Meneghwo. Gruffly picking splinters from between his claws and bits of what once were quilt from between his teeth, Black Rindle fumed. He had plenty of anger still for the spirit wolf, but a more potent fury burned within Black Rindle's breast. Though fully awake, he could not erase the stench and the nauseating taste of the Wyrm-taint. Grudgingly he conceded that Meneghwo had made his point: Black Rindle would not turn his back on the Wyrm-threat. He would not evade, would not rationalize. For the first time in his life, he felt the purest rage welling up from the innermost places of his heart, a rage that put the lie to all of his previous angers and hatreds, a rage that gave him reason to exist.

Chapter 23

Kaitlin walked with her hands stuffed deep into the pockets of her parka. She couldn't help glancing into the woods every few seconds. The murderous bay of bloodthirsty monsters echoed in her memory if not in her ears. With each step along the road, she expected a massive, snarling wolf-creature, a werewolf, to lunge out of the forest and tear her limb from limb. Black Rindle had barely managed to protect her last night—just long enough for the Quilt Wolf to show up. Meneghwo. Spirit wolf. The other beasts had appeared chastened by his words of admonishment—but for how long? They didn't seem the most reasonable type. Kaitlin tried to shift her thoughts from the fangs and the claws and the blood that had splattered across her face in the darkness of the basement, but there were plenty of other grim thoughts to dwell upon.

Black Rindle was talking about leaving. That should have been a relief. Should have been, but wasn't. Her reluctance to see him go was purely a matter of physical safety, she kept telling herself. He had drawn the attention of those monsters to her; with him gone, what was to keep them from killing her? The Quilt Wolf might not show up next time. That concern, she wanted to believe, was the reason she felt uneasy about his going.

Maybe she had some fanciful idea about bringing together the worlds she couldn't seem to avoid. She had to reestablish her place in the mundane world, the normal world; she was trying to do that. But the world of the supernatural seemed adamant that it had some claim upon her. It wasn't going to let her go. If there was a chance that being with Black Rindle could reconcile those two worlds, like an offering to the spirits...

But that was foolish. Stupid.

There was certainly nothing of the personal in her reluctance to see him go. Nothing to do with loneliness, with days and nights shared with a fellow exile, nothing of sympathy, nothing of...

Certainly not.

He'd asked her to go away with him, but she'd rejected that out of hand. She'd had to. Before she'd thought about it too much, before she'd let herself *want* to go with him. She'd done too much running away already. That's what this place was: the farthest she could run. But she'd come to the end of that road, had turned around and was trying to work her way back. She couldn't start running all over again.

That was why she'd snuck out. She resented the fact that she needed to sneak out of her own house, but Black Rindle had to make up his own mind. She'd woken up just after noon and taken the risk of looking in on him—he'd been sleeping, but restlessly—then she'd left. If he was there when she got back, then they'd figure out what to do from there. If he was gone...then fine. Either way, she wasn't going to give up her home.

He'd shown her what he meant by *Wyrm-taint*. She didn't understand it, didn't begin to comprehend what had happened last night. But she knew that something was wrong, and she knew that something foul and dangerous was leaking from beneath the lab. Maybe Floyd could help. Kaitlin didn't know how to try to explain it to him. She wouldn't be able to show him what Black Rindle had shown her; she couldn't grab her boss and yank him through to some other world. But there had to be a way. Black Rindle might be ready to cut and run, but she wasn't.

Kaitlin looked back over her shoulder. The forest, with its winter-stripped trees and tangled underbrush, loomed ominous and grey. What seemed like so long ago, she had decided that she could never live in a city again, not knowing what she might encounter on any given block, any given day. Now she wondered if she'd ever again be able to feel comfortable in the wilds, or if the bloodthirsty howls would forever echo in her mind.

Black Rindle crouched low behind the fallen tree. The road—and Kaitlin—were closer than fifty yards ahead. She was going back to that place. Despite what he'd shown her. He stifled a growl deep in his throat, while his claws worked deep troughs into the dead trunk.

The girl was skittish. She kept looking back over her shoulder, this way and that. Black Rindle could not overcome his dismay that she would betray him. Why else would she go back, knowing what she knew? He pictured himself chasing her down and pouncing, laying her tiny body to waste. The thought both thrilled and sickened him. He'd awoken from his dream driven by rage against the Despoiler. The warrior in him wanted to strike the girl down—but he was tempered in his wrath by the words and actions of Meneghwo. The spirit wolf had said that Kaitlin was not the enemy, had lifted her up from the floor. Surely he wouldn't have done that if she were tainted.

Black Rindle didn't know what to think, except that he had other matters to attend to. He would have to discover the truth about Kaitlin later—if there was a later.

He took one last look at her, then turned away and headed deeper into the forest, moving quickly but not at a full run.

Having chosen his course of action, Black Rindle listened only to his furiously pounding heart, lest he begin to reconsider. He proceeded as if wearing blinders, shielding his eyes and his mind as well, focusing on only the most immediate future. Each step became a task of complete and unwavering concentration. He let his hatred of the Wyrm propel him; that sentiment was unquestionable. He sniffed at the stench he imagined still clung to him from his dream. There was room only for certainty: hatred of corruption, battle, life or death. He could not hazard thoughts that might cause him to question, that might turn his feet from this path. His single-mindedness might fray if he allowed his mind to wander. He had no time for the girl who had rejected him, who might very well have betrayed him; he had no energy to spare for those who had condemned and scorned him all his life; he had not tears left for his departed mother, for himself or his predicament.

He was a protector of Gaia, Ahroun, warrior born. His entire essence he gave over to hatred of the Wyrm, of corruption. The need of the people was so much larger than himself that he shrank to insignificance beside it. His entire life to this point had been a process of loss, and now he had nothing left to lose. He would save the land or die in the attempt—and he could not save the land by himself.

He chose each step as if it might be his last, taking note of every leaf, every twig, because if he paused, the wall that was his resolve might well begin to crumble.

Black Rindle crossed over the boundary that marked the bawn of the Sept of the Wailing Glade. In the very back of his mind, he expected to be called out, attacked. But he continued on, and no one raised voice against him. The spirit guardians did not yet regard him as an enemy, or perhaps, as Menegwho had pointed out and what Black Rindle had seen seemed to confirm, the spirits had indeed fled the caern.

Then he *heard*, riding on the cold evening wind, the wail of the sept. This was no baleful cry of a Wyrm-creature, as in EveSong's story; rather the voices of the people were joined as one, lamenting, remembering, honoring. The Dirge of the Fallen drew Black Rindle forward. Exile or no, he was born of this caern, of this sept, of this people. He listened to the howling voices and images they painted of Frederich Night Terror, of his life and of his deeds, but the dirge despite the specific notes of history could just as easily have been for Galia Rainchild, or for Black Rindle. Or, he thought, for Evert Cloudkill.

Following the low, mournful tenor of the dirge, Black Rindle approached the fire ring. The warmth of coals radiated beyond the clearing, though the funeral bier was burned almost completely to the ground. Six wolves sat in a semicircle, their snouts and voices raised to the heavens. Each of them wore his or her freshly won scars from last night's fight, as did Black Rindle. In his rage-form, he stood easily three times as high as the others, but he was not here to renew the battle.

Standing behind them, he added his own howl to the dirge. Not that Black Rindle had ever liked Night Terror — Frederich had consistently been one of the most dismissive of the metis — but an Ahroun struck down in service of Gaia warranted honor and praise.

One by one, as the others noticed the voice of the newcomer joined with their own, they fell silent. Claudia Stands Firm was the first to hear him. She faced him, shifted to woman-form, and placed hand to the klaive at her belt. EveSong and Cloudkill noticed next, their howls falling away to nothing. Finally Shreds Birch and Cynthia Slack Ear, Night Terror's fellow hunters, looked beyond their grief and saw Black Rindle. Almost at once, their songs shifted from homage to hostility, growls and snarling taking the place of the mournful notes. They rose from all fours, growing tall, muscular, powerful, their wolf-forms stretching and changing to that of Crinos.

Black Rindle's howl was the last to die. He did not have a practiced or attractive voice, but there was nothing in his wolfsong of sarcasm or resentment. Despite his personal feelings about Night Terror, he paid honest tribute to the fallen Garou. This alone seemed to stay the hand of the others.

"Haven't you done enough, Hunch?" EveSong snarled.

Black Rindle ignored the tale-teller, looking instead at Stands Firm. The Warder, like last night, watched him intently but seemed disinclined to pounce without provocation. Of course, Black Rindle's very presence, his mere existence, might prove to be provocation enough. Shreds Birch and Cynthia were ready to take up the struggle again, though Shreds Birch held one arm tight against her body, useless after last night, and slow to heal, as were the savage wounds of Garou teeth or claws.

"I have come back," Black Rindle said, as calmly as was possible in the snarling Garou tongue, "because the land is in need. There is Wyrm-taint that must be cleansed. You will listen to me."

A hush fell over the assembly. They were taken aback by Black Rindle's confidence and poise, his strength of bearing, metis or no. He met their glares one at a time, and his only thought was of the war that must be waged—not against his people, but against the Wyrm. He was Gaia's warrior. The present need was all consuming, the past a thing that for the moment did not exist, forgotten if not forgiven. Black Rindle's gaze seemed to calm them. Shreds Birch and Slack Ear no longer growled, perhaps remembering the Ahroun who had stood bravely against dire odds last night. Barks-at-Shadows glanced nervously at the others; he would follow their lead. EveSong watched Black Rindle suspiciously. And Evert Cloudkill...

The alpha shifted from wolf to man-form, and for a moment Black Rindle's resolve wavered. This was his father, the great crescent moon who had for so many years disavowed and spurned his metis offspring. Black Rindle felt himself shrink in stature; his hump was suddenly a leaden weight trying to bear him to the ground. This was his father, who he had shamed. Black Rindle felt the urge to fling himself down, to roll over and expose his belly in submission...but then he looked more closely.

And he saw the old, tired man that his father had become. Cloudkill's deep wrinkles had once been a sign of wisdom; now they looked like nothing more than loose skin hanging from a withering frame. His eyes, before always piercing emeralds, were pale and listless. Grief had eaten away at this proud Garou. Perhaps scorn and resentment had taken a toll as well, as they had on Black Rindle for so many years. He looked at his sad, weakened father and saw the worst aspects of himself: pride, denial.

"The stream is being corrupted," Black Rindle said. "Wyrm-taint working its way to the caern. And whether because of that or some other reason, Owl and Water Snake have turned their backs. We have failed them."

Cloudkill cringed. He turned his head and would not face his accuser. Black Rindle was shocked. Never before had he seen such...such *weakness* in his father. This could not be the renowned alpha, the crescent moon who had founded the sept. Black Rindle couldn't help the glimmer satisfaction of satisfaction he felt at seeing this man, who for so many years had derided and abused him, laid low. But Black Rindle saw, too, the sickness of Cloudkill reflected in the sickness of the land: the caern devoid of spirit guardians, the nearby stream increasingly corrupted by the foul excretions of the Wyrm. This never could have happened if Cloudkill weren't...

"Negligent," Black Rindle pronounced. "You've neglected your duties, old man. The spirits know. They've turned their back on you. Once Galia died, no one remained who was worthy of them."

Again, Cloudkill cringed. The other Garou, unused to their alpha receiving such harsh words, looked on in amazement, in anger. Shreds Birch, incensed, started forward, but Claudia Stands Firm stopped her with a single light touch on the arm. The Warder gave Black Rindle no other sign of encouragement. Perhaps she thought it was Cloudkill's right, his *duty*, to settle this matter.

"He mocks you, Evert," EveSong said through clenched teeth to his alpha. "This abomination, this metis runt who you suffered to live through pure charity—he mocks you."

Cloudkill would not respond. In truth, he seemed unable to respond, and the other Garou watched with rising confusion. All except EveSong, who grew angrier with each passing moment.

"He is an exile, Evert," said the tale-teller. "Say the word and we will destroy him." Muttered growls of approval rose from Shreds Birch.

"Have you forgotten the words of the Patchwork Wolf?" Black Rindle asked. "Garou does not kill Garou. There is Wyrm-taint in the land. *That* is our enemy."

"Say the word!" EveSong urged Cloudkill.

"Have you also forgotten," Black Rindle asked with growing confidence as the others hesitated, "who gave you those wounds, EveSong? I'll give you more if you force me to."

EveSong ignored the taunting. He turned instead to Cloudkill. "This is the one who killed Galia," he said. "His taint sickened her, rotted her away until she died."

The mention of Galia Rainchild brought about a marked change in Cloudkill. He whipped his face around to face for the first time Black Rindle. The alpha's eyes flashed fire.

"He killed her," EveSong said, feeding the fire. "As sure as he's standing here now, he killed her. She'd still be alive if it weren't for him."

Black Rindle had heard the charges many times before. He'd been accused of so many crimes over the years that his first inclination was to believe what the others said of him. He *was* the accursed of Gaia. He *was* a blight upon the land. His confidence, his determination began to backslide. Before him, Cloudkill suddenly appeared not so old as Black Rindle had thought, not so tired and weak.

"He killed Galia," EveSong repeated, "and he consorts with those who killed Frederich, humans who see us and hate us. If Hunch smells the stink of the Wyrm, it is because he is so close to it, corrupted himself since the day he was born."

"Are you not exiled?" Cloudkill demanded, standing tall now, balling his hands into fists at his sides. "Was I too merciful before?"

Lurking beneath his own dwindling resolve, Black Rindle felt the urge to flee. He faced again the father of his childhood, a giant among Garou, who had banished the Wyrm and made a safe haven of this place. But the Wyrm was *not* banished, Black Rindle told himself. That was the problem, but no one would acknowledge it. Yet he was surrounded by those hostile to him, those who had always known him and saw that he was not Gaia's warrior but her accursed. Nothing Meneghwo said could change that.

Gradually, tauntingly slowly, Evert Cloudkill shifted from man-from to great white-streaked Crinos. Black Rindle was larger, but he felt a cub again, a disobedient child having angered his elder.

"There is not taint," Cloudkill snarled. "No taint but you."

Black Rindle had not given any ground, but he was on the verge of panic. As he met his father's fierce gaze, Black Rindle saw nothing of rage in the green eyes—only violent, bloodthirsty hate. *Rage and hatred are not one and the same*, Owl had said. *You must rely on the first without surrendering yourself to the second.* Black Rindle drew strength from the spirit wisdom.

His entire life he had not lived in accordance with those words. But neither had the others. Neither had Cloudkill. The alpha had hated Black Rindle as long as the metis could remember. Maybe their treatment of him had been justified, maybe not. But tonight Black Rindle was here to fight for the future, not to fight again the lost battles of the past.

"I have come," Black Rindle said, "so that the Garou might cleanse this land of the taint you will not even admit exits. You are no longer fit to lead the Sept of the Wailing Glade, Evert Cloudkill. I challenge you."

"There will be no challenge, you abomination," Cloudkill snarled. "I have been merciful to you for the last time." He raised a fist to the heavens and roared to his followers: "Kill him! Rid us of his pestilence."

Black Rindle readied himself for attacks from every direction—but no attack came. Claudia Stands Firm still held the arm of Shreds Birch, who was ready to move forward. Cynthia Slack Ear and Barks-at-Shadows looked to the other two.

EveSong started forward but stopped when he realized that the others were not attacking. "There will be no spirit wolf to save him tonight," EveSong said, trying to urge on the others.

"Garou does not kill Garou," Stands Firm said. "A challenge has been issued. The good of the caern demands that it be addressed."

"He is exiled!" EveSong insisted.

Stands Firm did not budge, and the others were too shocked to move against her. Never before had she stood against the alpha.

For all of EveSong's cursing and exhorting, Cloudkill, strangely enough, reacted more calmly. When the attack did not fall, and it was apparent that the Warder considered Black Rindle's challenge valid, Cloudkill slowly lowered his fist.

"Strike him down!" EveSong cried to his alpha. "If it weren't for him, Galia would still be alive!"

But the specter of Galia Rainchild had lost its potency, and likewise Cloudkill his will to resist.

Black Rindle, heartened by Claudia's support—in his cause, if not in him—moved toward his father. "Stand down, Evert." Cloudkill, robbed of his passion, still snarled and bared his teeth. "Stand down," Black Rindle said again, holding in check his desire to lash this Garou from one end of the caern to the other. That was not the purpose of the challenge. "Stand down, and we can battle the Wyrm together…father."

It was the first time in his life that Black Rindle had called Evert that in the elder's presence. For a moment they faced one another, gazed locked. Then Cloudkill spat in Black Rindle's eye, and slashed him across the face.

Black Rindle staggered back. He put a hand to his cheek, then for several seconds stared at the blood drawn by his own sire. Hatred and triumph twisted Cloudkill's face. "Be gone," he said, "or there will be no more mercy."

Black Rindle stepped forward again. "You have *never* shown me mercy," he said. He wanted to say more—there was so much to say, so much he could never say—but the challenge was not about the past but the future. The future from this point onward. Black Rindle drew back his hand and struck a single mighty blow.

Cloudkill left his feet, propelled by the strike that left his chest and face open and bleeding. He came to rest on his back near the stream. For a moment he tried to rise, but his will deserted him. Struck down by his own folly, the indignity and shame were more than he could bear. He lay still in the dirt.

The others stared at Black Rindle in silence. He returned their gazes, slowly looking from one to the next to the next. Over his shoulder to Cloudkill he said: "You can stay if you will fight the Wyrm with me. Otherwise be gone from here." He faced the other Garou again. "The same for you all. Accept my leadership or leave."

Claudia Stands Firm stepped toward him. In woman-form still, she bowed her head to him. "I have served as Warder for...too long to recount. I grew complacent, as did we all, and would not see the sickness that should have been clear. I have failed my sept and the spirits. I have failed the Garou. I have failed Gaia. And so I step down so that you may name a Warder of your choice."

"I would choose no other than you," Black Rindle said without hesitation. "We have all had our own failings, but from tonight we will be tireless. We will make ourselves worthy of the spirits attentions and friendship." In a challenge to the Wyrm, Black Rindle raised his howl to Sister Luna, who was still rising in the night sky. One by one the others joined him: Claudia Stands Firm, and Barks-at-Shadows, and then Shreds Birch, and Cynthia Slack Ear.

As their voices entwined, one amongst the others, EveSong helped Cloudkill to his feet, and the two of them staggered away into the cold.

Curious about other Crossroad Press books? Stop by our
website: http://crossroadpress.com
We offer quality writing
in digital, audio, and print formats.

Subscribe to our newsletter on the website homepage and
receive a free eBook.